SLEEP WITH SLANDER

DOLORES HITCHENS

SLEEP WITH SLANDER

WITH A FOREWORD BY
STEPH CHA

LIBRARY OF AMERICA

Published by the Library of America.
Visit our website at www.loa.org.

Cover and text design by Donna G. Brown.
Composition by Dianna Logan.

Distributed to the trade in the United States by
Penguin Random House Inc. and in Canada by
Penguin Random House Canada Ltd.

Library of Congress Control Number: 2020951990

ISBN 978-1-59853-698-0

1 3 5 7 9 10 8 6 4 2

Printed in the United States of America

CONTENTS

Foreword by Steph Cha   xi

Sleep with Slander   I

About Dolores Hitchens and Steph Cha   227

FOREWORD

The woman born Julia Clara Catherine Maria Dolores Robins wrote dozens of novels under four names: the pseudonyms D. B. Olsen, Dolan Birkley, Noel Burke, and, of course, her second married name, Dolores Hitchens. She was a prolific writer with the kind of range that might necessitate multiple pen names, traipsing around the genre with agility and bravado throughout a career that spanned decades—from the 1938 publication of *The Clue in the Clay* to her death in 1973. Her Rachel Murdock series, which featured a spinster detective with a feline sidekick, was an early example of the cat mystery subgenre, now firmly associated with cozy mysteries. Her two James Sader books, *Sleep with Strangers* (1955) and *Sleep with Slander* (1960), lie at the opposite end of the crime spectrum. They are moody, chewy, hard-boiled detective novels with a male private investigator protagonist.

Hitchens was not remarkable because she was a woman, but it would be willful and silly to discuss her legacy, and these novels in particular, without taking her gender into account. Even now, almost fifty years after Hitchens's death, gender and genre remain stubbornly intertwined in crime fiction. Cozy mysteries are written, for the most part, by and for women and ignored or dismissed by male readers and critics to a proportionate degree. Meanwhile, private eye fiction is dominated by men and male arche-types, so much so that female authors in this subgenre are often defined by our difference—our work seen, if not as masculine, as explicitly counter-masculine. It is un-surprising that Bill Pronzini, in praising *Sleep with Slan-der*, described it as "the best traditional male private eye novel written by a woman" before adding, "and one of the best written by anybody." Pronzini won the Private Eye Writers of America's inaugural Shamus Award for Best P.I. Hardcover Novel in 1982. Only seven female writers have won this award (for a total of ten wins—three for Sue Grafton and two for S. J. Rozan).

There is certainly something traditional about James Sader—he's a sleuth with a moral compass that doesn't depend on law, and he deals with both femmes fatale and alcoholism. Like Philip Marlowe and Lew Archer, he roams around Southern California, burning through shoe leather and pissing people off. His domain is Long Beach, "the town that had grown up from a village by the sea, a city with a hill in the middle of it, sprouting oil derricks like a forest of pins."

We meet Sader in *Sleep with Strangers*, when he visits his new client, Kay Wanderley, "a slender, well-shaped girl with blonde hair." We see him after we see her: "The man on the step was in the act of lighting a cigarette. Rain lay in his hair, which was hatless, and which also, though obviously once reddish, now had faded to a tawny rust laced with gray. He had a lean, sharp, intelligent face. The hands that cupped the match wore a look of mobile strength."

As he tells another woman, "Detectives aren't half as glamorous in real life as they are on TV, or in the movies," and this is true of Sader, who fumbles through both novels without the benefit of any special charisma or genius. What he does have are the plain, well-worn tools of integrity and tenacity, scuffed by age and alcoholism. Unlike the typical boozed-up private eye, Sader is, for the most part, a sober drunk. "I'm a high-dive drinker," he explains. "That first taste of alcohol is the same as jumping off a ten-story building. I'd like to get back up, but I can't." While his relationship with alcohol never takes over the story—no destructive benders, no Alcoholics Anonymous —it's a thread that runs through both novels, taut and threatening as a tripwire. Our man is, at baseline, in a constant struggle for control, and he spends all his time running down liars, cheaters, and killers.

In *Sleep with Strangers*, Sader grapples with a sordid, depressing case about money and corruption that directly recalls Raymond Chandler's *The Big Sleep*. There's a rich old man, a few young, wayward women—even a pivotal oil sump. But while his streets are just as mean, Sader is a shabbier hero than Marlowe:

> He'd been young once, yes; but that was over. It was really and finally over. The bitter truth was that he

was now a tired man with gray in his hair, with the beginning of a stoop, and no amount of frenzy or cunning, no wishing . . . could bring back that which had gone forever. There must be a time like this in everyone's life, he thought numbly. When all your illusions go down the drain. When you see at last what you have lost.

Sader develops an infatuation with Kay, and in one of the novel's wackier episodes, he more or less abducts her, taking her to Vegas to hide away and possibly marry, against her will and for what he mistakenly believes is her own good. Marlowe—who threw a young, willing, naked Carmen Sternwood out of his bed—would never have acted so desperate.

But Sader's flaws and foibles make him a compelling character, worth following as he wanders around Long Beach looking for answers, digging until he hits the truth. He solves the case, but there's more to it than that. His investigation leads him to a forceful confrontation with reality, as well as the pain of adapting to that reality. Kay Wanderley offers a similar theory about her missing mother: "She had a world that she loved and it fell apart, and then she was lost. She was like a child alone in the dark."

Sleep with Slander is more or less literally about a child alone in the dark. Sader is hired by Hale Gibbings, a wealthy sixty-year-old architect, who tells him, "I need most of all an honest man. Yes . . . a kind of crook, and yet honest." Gibbings asks him to track down a five-year-old boy being abused by an unknown party in an unknown place. Sader doesn't trust his client and his task proves remarkably frustrating, with even the most basic facts about the child and his origins proving difficult to pin down.

> There was something inside the amorphous case, a hard core he couldn't quite get a grip on. He tried to think of a comparison and remembered something his grandmother had said once, something about a flatiron inside a feather bed. There was a flatiron somewhere inside this thing but he couldn't find it. He just knew that it was there. A booby trap.

The case twists and plunges admirably, and through it all, Sader holds on, propelled by a simple core of decency and the fact of this suffering child: "You couldn't endure thinking of the child's body subjected to abuse; the tears were warm and wet, and the sobs were something you heard if you stopped to listen." Pronzini was right: *Sleep with Slander* should be a classic of the private investigator genre. It has the breadth and the depth, the memorable characters, the vivid style, and the brutal emotional impact of the best hard-boiled detective fiction.

Of course, Hitchens had some of the blind spots you might expect of a white American writer of her era. Almost all of the characters in these books are white, and when they're not, the difference is very much noted. A "chocolate-colored maid" appears and disappears within a sentence; a half-Asian supporting character in *Sleep with*

Strangers has a larger part, but every time she shows up, we hear about her "exotic, oriental eyes." To be fair, Long Beach was, as of the 1950 census, 97.4 percent white. These days, it's a majority minority city that's given us Snoop Dogg and a vibrant Cambodia Town, the largest ethnically Cambodian community outside of Cambodia. It also has a new literary sleuth: Joe Ide's Isaiah Quintabe, a brilliant Black detective in the Sherlock Holmes tradition, presiding over the bustling life of contemporary Long Beach.

But Ide's work doesn't overwrite Hitchens's any more than mine overwrites Chandler's. *Sleep with Strangers* and *Sleep with Slander* capture a different era of Long Beach's history, and Sader is the perfect guide—a dogged private investigator who muddles through darkness, "realizing that the city in which he had grown up had a side to it he had never known," and shining light wherever he goes.

Steph Cha
Los Angeles, November 2020

SLEEP WITH SLANDER

He turned tiptoeing from the refrigerator, the bottle of milk cold and slippery in his grasp. The little light shone out upon the dark floor, painted the long shadow of his legs against the kitchen wall. He moved with watchful care toward the table, but then he heard a sudden noise, and started, and the bottle fell rolling, with milk spreading like a ghostly lake.

He waited trembling, a hand over his mouth. A shadow came in at the door, and he whimpered. A shape in a wrapper loomed over him; hands gripped his shoulders and the shaking started, so hard that it seemed his head must snap from his neck, and his senses swam.

"You brat! You dirty horrible little brat!"

One hand lifted from his shoulder and the slapping began. He tried to crouch, to protect his head. All of his insides knotted and drew small, his body trying to curl itself into the fetal cocoon. But he was yanked straight, a hand gripping his hair. The screams he had tried to contain burst free.

He fell, and something kicked him. The spilled milk felt cold and clammy in his clothes. He was dragged through it, knowing where he was headed now, begging not to be put there.

The musty closed-in smell reached out for him, and he tried to brace his legs at the sill; but this was useless. He was flung in and the closet door was slammed, the key turned. He was alone and it was very dark.

After a while, when there were no more tears, he felt around for the folded bit of carpet, crawled upon it and curled himself, and shut his eyes. He sucked his thumb for a while, and finally went to sleep. There were coats on the rack above, and he was cold, but he had no thought of covering with them. They belonged to the others.

The house creaked and whispered to itself, and the night wore away. When it was almost dawn there were soft steps in the hall outside the closet door, and a sharp, listening silence. The boy in the closet was unaware, far gone in dreams. When he awoke there would be again hunger, and the strange implacable anger that waited like a toying cat, and blows, and the unbelief with which he regarded his five-year-old world.

But for this moment, there was peace.

CHAPTER ONE

The sign on the door that let into the corridor said SADER AND SCARBOROUGH, PRIVATE DETECTIVES.

Sader was in the inner office looking over some glossy photos of an automobile accident and its victims. He stood behind his desk, the photos laid out on it; he was a little stooped in posture, taking something from his height. He was smoking a cigarette. He was a lean man with hair that had once been red and now had grayed to rust, with intelligent eyes and an air of patience. When the bell pealed in the outer room he crushed the cigarette into an abalone-shell tray and went to answer. On his way he glanced at the clock. It was not quite nine-thirty, a misty morning in October, with dark skies threatening to rain.

He opened the door. In the hall was a man in a weather-proof overcoat, muffler, brown felt hat, overshoes. He was about sixty, Sader thought. He had a snow-white mustache and eyes like two steel rivets. "You're the detective?" he demanded, in Sader's opinion rather louder than necessary. "Are you any good?"

"I'm busy," Sader said, losing the air of patience.

"Busy?"

"My partner's on vacation and I have about all the work I can handle."

"Made you mad." The pale lips parted in a grin. The dentist had fitted him with small, even teeth and in the rugged face they were ridiculous. "Makes you mad for someone to want to know if you're any good?"

Sader controlled what he wanted to say, stepped back. "Come in, please."

The old man paused in the outer office, reached under the overcoat and got out a wallet, extracted a business card and handed it to Sader. The card read:

FRIMM, WATLEY AND STONE
ARCHITECTS
4900 Wilshire Boulevard   Los Angeles, California

Sader read the card and looked up. "You're Mr. Frimm?"

"I'm not any of them. They're all dead. Started the firm in L.A. in eighteen seventy. My name is Gibbings. Hale Gibbings."

"You *are* an architect?"

"Senior partner now." Gibbings was looking around at the outer room, which was empty except for a water cooler and some filing cabinets. "Do we talk here or can we sit down?"

"We can sit down." Sader ushered him into the other office. Two big desks were placed back to back, there were several chairs and a thick rug and a leather couch. Sader quickly shuffled the accident photos into a stack and dropped them into a drawer. He placed Gibbings' card in the exact center of the desk. Gibbings was seated on the couch. "Now. What can I do for you?"

The old man opened the overcoat and stretched his legs —as if, Sader thought, the joints might be just a little rheumatic. He was staring at Sader with the steel-rivet eyes, no humor in his face. "How good are you, really? No, don't get sore! I guess I should have said, what kind of an operator are you? I've got to have a certain kind of man. A certain touch. I need a weasel, an opportunist, somebody with the mind of a shakedown artist. A corner-cutter. Even . . . you might say . . . a kind of pimp."

Sader felt himself stiffen, and he was aware of a faint apprehension. Gibbings looked as cool as a floating hawk, but Sader didn't like this beginning and he wondered if he should ask him to leave before anything more was said.

"You *look* like you've been around." Gibbings had taken out a pipe and was fussing with it. "At the same time that I need all these things," he went on as if continuing his previous specifications, "I need most of all an honest man. Yes . . . a kind of crook, and yet honest." He got a match lighted; it flared between his fingers. "Do you see what I mean?"

"I'm afraid not, no, sir."

"How much of a—" He waved the pipe as if including Sader with the office furnishings. "—of a code, or ethics, or standard of behavior do you have to keep to, in these places? Do you have to account to anyone for what you do? Some licensing committee?"

"Some private detectives get away with quite a bit, for quite a while," Sader said. "I guess it depends on the individual. We are licensed by the state and we are expected to co-operate with other law-enforcement bodies. Does that answer your question?"

"What about you? How do you run things?"

"We don't ordinarily do divorce work," Sader told him. This didn't seem to make the difference he had expected. "We do a lot of looking for missing people. Not skip-tracing, there are much bigger outfits doing that. We look for heirs, and people who have run away from law suits, and sometimes accident victims. We are occasionally called on by defense attorneys to find evidence for their clients. We—"

Gibbings waved the pipe again. "No, what I mean is, are you a sharp boy? Do you push? Can you hound and harry and finagle?"

"I guess you'd better tell me what it's all about."

Gibbings frowned, then nodded. The pipe had an alfalfa-and-haymow smell, not at all unpleasant. "Well . . . this is in confidence, of course."

"Of course." Sader prepared himself to listen. "I might put in here, Mr. Gibbings, that I think you should be careful whom you select under these qualifications."

Gibbings grinned, showing the misplacedly small and even teeth. "I'll be cautious . . . even now, with you. The job I need a man for concerns a child. My daughter bore a child out of wedlock—silly phrase—five years ago. She was in love with a young man and before they could marry he was drafted into the Army and sent to Japan, where he died of a fever." Gibbings paused and waited as if to see how Sader was taking it.

Sader wondered fleetingly why it seemed so often to be dirty linen which was brought to him. Why couldn't he be asked, once, to run down a missing masterpiece? A first edition Milton or a Van Gogh? Or a stolen Stradivarius? Something cultural and elevating. "And the baby?"

"It was given out for adoption."

"Through a recognized adoption agency?"

Gibbings shook his head, his expression one of sudden dour gloom. He began to feel around in an inside coat pocket. "This hasn't a damned thing to do with that angle. The adoption was private, legal, all in order, a nice couple— I saw to that." He had found an envelope. It looked tattered as if from a great deal of handling. Gibbings took a sheet of paper from it, handed it to Sader. "This came through the mail almost a week ago. At first I wasn't inclined to do anything about it. But then I found that it was preying on my mind. Now I find it hard to get to sleep at night and my appetite's getting finicky."

Sader swung around so the light shone on the page. There was no salutation; the body of the letter began abruptly about two inches below the top of the sheet. It was typewritten, the ribbon quite pale and the over-all appearance of the lettering spotty because of uneven pressure on the keys.

You ought to try to do something about the child who was once your daughter's own little baby. The people you gave him to are dead and he has been taken by a relative of theirs. He is treated just terrible in that house. He goes hungry most of the time, almost starving. He is whipped and spanked every day, sometimes several times a day, and for any old reason at all, or over nothing. They don't send him to kindergarten. They don't let him play with the other children. I wouldn't bother you, but I really don't think he is going to live much longer. I think he will die.

I could tell you the address now and maybe you'd go there and maybe you wouldn't. After all, you are the one who gave him away to strangers when he was little and helpless. So I won't tell you the address, and if you care enough you can find it and do something about him.

And if you show this letter to that woman you'll just get me into trouble, too, and she can make plenty.

"The perversity," Gibbings declared, "the utterly pig-headed perversity of this creature, denying me the address—"

Sader held up a hand, shutting him off. Sader went back through the letter, reading it under his breath to himself, pausing here and there to re-examine a phrase. Then he sat looking at the window. Finally he glanced again at Gibbings. "Of course you have done some preliminary work on your own, you tried to trace these people, find out if they were really dead and to whom they might have given the boy."

"Naturally I did what I could, I went as far as I was able. I found out that the man of the couple, the adopted father, was killed in an airplane crash. A big airliner. Fell in

Colorado. They brought him back to L.A. for burial. Happened two years ago. The baby was three, then."

"Tell me about this couple."

Gibbings made an impatient gesture. "They were just an ordinary, decent young couple. The name was Champlain. French descent, I think. He was an engineer for an electronics research outfit, made good money, must have had a pretty good brain. She'd been a schoolteacher. They wanted a baby very badly and couldn't have one."

"How did you contact them?"

"I didn't. They came to see me. Kit's time was about up and I'd been thinking of asking the doctor about getting foster parents, or perhaps throwing a hint to my attorney. The Champlains said they had heard we might have a baby for adoption, and they wanted to offer their credentials, or whatever. They came to my office, during office hours, and they were very nice but businesslike, and I took to them both."

"You had them investigated?"

Gibbings' flow of words was stifled and he shifted his legs, moving about as if in discomfort. "Well, no. He had documents with him, their birth certificates and their marriage license, a lot of stuff about their house mortgage and the pink slips on their two cars, plus a couple of letters, one from a banker and one from a minister. You could see they were a nice little family, solid and decent and kindly."

"But not immortal."

Gibbings gave him a hard stare. "You're a wisecracker, huh?"

"Your answer to that one should have been that even

real parents can't be—everyone dies. You still haven't said anything to account for the kind of man you say you're looking for. The semi-crook."

"I'm coming to it." Gibbings' glance was flinty; he was obviously beginning to dislike Sader heartily. "Kit had a friend, a girl named Wanda Nevins, and from things which happened afterward I got the idea that she was the one who had sent the Champlains to me. She had told them about Kit's coming baby, and I have no doubt that she charged them for the information. They were pretty desperate, and she was . . . is . . . the kind who wouldn't give you the time of day without a price tag on it."

Sader looked at the old man thoughtfully. "It's through her, then, that you think I'll have to go to find the child."

"She knows," Gibbings agreed.

"She offered to tell you for a price?"

Again the air of discomfort and self-reproach appeared on Gibbings' seamed face. "I blew my stack. I haven't any use for her or for her kind and I let her know it."

Sader had put the letter on the desk beside Gibbings' card. He made a gesture toward it. "Had it occurred to you that she might be the one who sent you this?"

"I thought about that angle, yes. But it isn't the way Wanda would go about it if she wanted to get money out of me. She's much more direct. Besides—well, she wouldn't write that kind of letter, she wouldn't express any sympathy or concern for the child. She'd be matter-of-fact. She'd say, so-and-so is happening and if you pay me I'll see that it's stopped."

"By calling the cops? Why doesn't the writer of the letter

do just that, by the way? We have laws for the protection of children."

"All I know is what's in that letter," Gibbings snapped. "And if you're wondering why *I* didn't go to the cops, a moment's reflection might supply the answer."

"This involves something more important than your daughter's reputation. You're playing with a child's life."

"*If* the letter is true. Which it might well not be. I'm pretty well known in Southern California, there must be a lot of people who think I'm carrying it around in suitcases. This could be a shakedown."

"You've already eliminated the one you would expect to shake you down."

Gibbings' mouth seemed hard and mean. "Do you want the job, or don't you?"

Sader opened a desk drawer, slapped a writing pad on the desk, took a pen from his coat pocket. "Let's start with dates. The date the foster parents first came to see you. The date the baby was born. The date he was taken by the Champlains. And when Mr. Champlain died in the crash in Colorado."

Gibbings said, "There's one more thing to keep straight, before this goes any further. At no time—" He stopped and seemed to think over how to word what he wanted to say. "—at no time during your investigation are you to imply that the child you are looking for is the child of my daughter. Or that he is related to me."

"You really must think it's a shakedown," Sader said, looking at him curiously.

"Do you understand, Mr. Sader?"

"Yes, I understand. I am trying to trace the adopted child of the Champlains. Previous antecedents unknown."

"That is correct, sir."

Sader thought, What a stiff-necked old buzzard he is, putting up an additional safeguard against ever having to claim his grandson.

When Gibbings supplied the dates, Sader sat studying them. The Champlains had come to Gibbings' office in late August. The child had been born a little more than two weeks later, the middle of September five years back. He had been taken from the private maternity hospital four days after birth. To Sader it seemed a hurried and casual way to dispose of a grandchild, illegitimate or not. "Did you ever see the child?" he asked, glancing up at Gibbings.

The old man seemed intent on his pipe, which must have gone out. "Yes. Once. In the hospital nursery. I wanted to be sure that it was a normal baby, that there was nothing to prevent its adoption and complete family attachment to the Champlains."

"It was normal?"

"Quite normal and . . . a very good-looking baby."

"How old was your daughter?"

Gibbings squinted into the bowl of the pipe. "That, Mr. Sader, has nothing to do with any of this."

Sader felt a sudden suspicion, of which he said nothing. Gibbings must be at least sixty. It was quite possible that this daughter didn't fit into the rash-young-teenager-in-love pattern, at all. In fact, come to think of it, most proba-bly not. "I'll need addresses, now."

The Champlains had lived in West L.A. until the

father's death in the plane crash. Then Mrs. Champlain and the baby moved to Santa Monica. Why, Gibbings didn't know. He had been able to trace them through a friend in the Motor Vehicle Department, who had looked up Mrs. Champlain's changes of address through her driver's license. The Santa Monica address was the last listed.

"Mrs. Champlain is dead? You're sure of this?"

"I haven't been able to verify it. The father's death was mentioned in the papers at the time. I didn't see it, or at least the story didn't register if I did. A reporter friend looked it up in the newspaper morgue."

Sader was reading back through the notes he had made. "You said that they brought you letters of recommendation from a banker and a minister."

"Don't remember the banker. The minister was in a West L.A. church and I called them yesterday. The church says that he took a sabbatical leave more than three years ago and went back to some theological college in the South, and has stayed there since to teach." Gibbings frowned. "Anyway, he wasn't a personal friend. It's through others, the people close to them—"

Sader interrupted. "We may need that minister before we're through. What's the church?"

"A little outfit. The Lakeside Chapel of St. John's. Sort of interfaith bunch, don't believe they stick to many of the fundamentals."

"Perhaps they have their own," Sader suggested dryly.

"You'll be telling me next—" Gibbings tried to smile, and the effect was grim. "—telling me I'm not a Christian."

"Are you?"

"If you knew it all . . ." He shrugged the rest of it away. "Your best bet, take it from me, is to go to see Wanda Nevins. Don't let her know I sent you. You'll need every trick you ever learned. She lives down the coast, this side of Laguna Beach. She's got a house overlooking the sea, a Cadillac convertible, and two boxer dogs." Gibbings rose from the couch. "Don't let any of them get you." He slapped a small stack of money on the desk in front of Sader. "This ought to get you going."

He turned, buttoning the coat. He looked, Sader thought, like an old soldier who has seen too much of war.

CHAPTER TWO

The moment that Sader saw the place in Santa Monica, the last known address of Mrs. Champlain, he knew that this was a dead end . . . and why. Gibbings should have told him.

A new freeway was going through. An area of a dozen blocks or so had been condemned, the houses and shops were in the process of being moved or demolished. They sat with vacant windows under the darkly clouded sky. Some had been pried from their foundation and sat intact on timbers, ready for the rollers. On others the wreckers had been at work, steps were askew and doors and windows and all exterior fittings were gone. Here and there a tattered FOR SALE sign fluttered in the beach wind. Sader parked across the street and got out of the car. Three blocks east the end of the freeway from L.A. was a muddy mountainous nose thrust sniffing seaward.

He went to the address Gibbings had given him. It was one of those being wrecked, a small stucco bungalow with a Spanish tile roof. The low picket fence around the front yard had been flattened, lay in splinters on the dead lawn. A couple of hibiscus were trying to live without water, and even showed a few starved buds. Sader went into the shaky porch and looked in through the doorless entry. Someone had taken the hardwood, leaving the rough planked floor. The plastered walls were cracked. He went inside.

It didn't smell like a house. The windows were gone, and the beach wind lent it a salty fragrance. Under the salt was the faint odor of broken wood. No one had slept here, cooked here, washed and ironed here, or kept a baby here for a long long time.

It was as bare as a house could get. In the kitchen the sink had been ripped off the wall and taken away. The water heater lay on its side in the service porch, a trickle of rust like dried blood testifying to its uselessness. Who needed rusty water heaters? Sader looked for personal debris, for something left by the living tenants; and it seemed he would find nothing. The house had been scoured by human gleaners, and by time.

He went into the front bedroom. The hibiscus crowded the vacant window. He looked into the closet. Everywhere in the house the flooring was gone, the subfloor exposed, and through the cracks between the planks he could see the dark underneath. The closet had lost its smell of clothing. If anything, there was a faint odor of earth. He went past a gutted bathroom to the back bedroom. This should have been the baby's room, he thought. It was much smaller, a little box of a room. He looked into its closet, a veritable mousehole. Empty, too, to the cracked walls.

He went past the fallen water heater to the rear porch.

A broken screen door lay in the back yard, grass growing up through the wire mesh. There was nothing out there except a barrel, sitting crookedly beside an old incinerator. Sader picked his way through the yard, gathering foxtails in the cuffs of his pants, and looked into the incinerator, which proved to be clogged with ashes, and then into the barrel. In the bottom of the barrel, old newspapers had matted to the wood and on these sat a cardboard box. Sader picked it out.

It had been wet, rained on maybe. The white paper covering was cracked and spotted. He pried up the lid. Because it was so light to hold, he thought it must be empty; but no, inside was a crushed mass of satiny color and the smell of lavender. He stirred what was in the box. A lot of ribbon, yellow and pink and orchid and blue, and some scraps of lace. A baby's mitten, white, with a touch of pink at the wrist. A small locket on a chain, badly tarnished. Three pearl buttons. Some loose bits of lavender, from which the fragrance came.

He put the lid on again, saw that there had been a firm's name printed on it, almost blotted away by the water. He held it to the light and the last of the gilt print said *Betty's Baby Shop.*

He took the box with him to the house. He made a last inspection, peering into what was left of the kitchen cupboards. Then he returned to his car. He tossed the box in upon the seat, then paused on the curb to light a cigarette.

There was no proof whatever that the box had belonged to Mrs. Champlain. Gibbings claimed not to have been able to find out if she had lived here until her supposed death, or even when the death had occurred; and even if he had settled these items, in the present state of the neighborhood the box could have come from almost anywhere. Still, Sader glanced in at it with a look of satisfaction.

He looked at his wrist watch. It was almost noon.

He drove back to Long Beach, checked the office. There was a wire from his partner. The wire said THEY STILL KNOW HOW TO LIVE IT UP IN SAN FRANCISCO. PLEASE CHECK SUPPLY OF ALKA-SELTZER AND BUY ME A NEW ICE BAG. BE HOME WEDNESDAY. DON'T TAKE ANY WOODEN BLONDES. Sader dropped the telegram into the waste basket, phoned his answering service, found out he hadn't missed anything important, and went back down to his car.

He drove south, down the coast. The gray sea was the color of the sky, with flecks of foam, and Catalina was a sleeping armadillo on the horizon. He thought about this job Gibbings had sent him on, and all the territory Gibbings hadn't let him explore, everything that had to do with the daughter. The daughter didn't know about the letter, had no inkling that her child wasn't still with the Champlains —if she'd ever been allowed to know *that*. There was much under the surface and the old man wasn't going to let him touch it. In spite of the erosion done his natural curiosity by time and by being in the detective business, Sader felt an interest in the daughter. He wondered what she looked like. Was she beautiful and dumb? Was she a plain Jane whose one misstep had had such unfortunate consequences? Did she resemble her father—God forbid? He wondered what had really happened to her. That story of being in love with the soldier, for instance, and the soldier having been killed before the marriage could take place . . . Sader shook his head over it. It was as old as hell. He thought that a man with Gibbings' intelligence should have done better.

The old man should have been scarred and hurt by the experience, the scandal, but Sader thought not. Gibbings was a cold fish with an eye for his own interest.

There had been no mention of the girl's mother, Gibbings' wife, an omission Sader figured was deliberate. Probably with the way Gibbings had run things, she didn't even know there had been a baby.

When he got into the outskirts of Laguna, Sader began to watch for the street Gibbings had given him. He found it. It climbed the steep hill to a terrace where houses sat looking out across the sea. They were pretty big places. Under the gray light their big glass windows were milky, secretive. He found Wanda Nevins' number and parked beside the curb.

At street level was a paved courtyard, in its center like a hole in a doughnut a raised area of earth from which sprouted some banana palms and papyrus. Sader went in, looked around for the door. Between the house and the garage was an open passage through which, far below, he could see the water. The air was fresh and salty.

The door was set into the redwood wall. Sader put a thumb on the bell and waited. He heard radio music dimly, and then the noise of some movement inside. The door opened a little. "Miss Nevins?"

She was surprisingly little, her black curly head barely topping the level of his shoulder. She had fair clear skin,

21

the kind of skin the old-fashioned songs always compared to rose petals, and her tawny and insolent eyes looked directly into Sader's face. She was barefooted, dressed in some brief kind of sun suit, a burnt-toast shade that pointed up the color of her eyes. "Who are you and what do you want?"

"My name's Sader. I'd like to talk to you, if I might."

She studied him. Her expression made Sader feel worn and dusty, and conscious of being gray. "What's it all about?"

"A confidential matter. I can't very well explain standing out here. I promise not to take much of your time."

She glanced past him to the car, which apparently didn't impress her. "I don't entertain people I don't know. I don't know you, and I have no intention of letting you in my house."

While he took out his I.D., Sader thought to himself, This kid's been spoiled but good. For years and years people have stared at her because she's beautiful, and kowtowed to her and run themselves ragged trying to please her—men especially—and now she has the manners of a bitch. He flashed the private detective's badge and saw her eyes widen. Not in surprise. He would have bet on it. She seemed to pick up a lot of satisfied animation all at once.

"You're a cop?"

"I'm a private investigator."

"That's an official-looking badge."

"I can be pretty official when it's necessary," Sader said. "May I come inside?"

She didn't move, but the insolent eyes had taken on a new curiosity. "Who sent you here?"

"I'm employed by a group of attorneys who look up heirs, Miss Nevins." It was the truth, and Sader often found it convenient as a cover. "Right now we're hunting for a Mrs. Champlain, or a son of hers."

In the lovely face the brown eyes seemed unnaturally fixed and steady. "On account of an inheritance? You mean there's money coming to them?"

"If we can find them," Sader agreed.

The door promptly opened and she stepped back. Sader took in the room beyond. It looked bigger than it really was —and it was big enough—because of the Oriental sparseness of furniture. The gray light from the windows overlooking the sea shone in on teakwood benches, fiber mats, transparent paper screens and squat-sized tables holding bonsai pine trees in copper bowls. Over by the windows with his back to the view was the biggest household Buddha that Sader had ever encountered face to face. He had his own teakwood perch and a look of brooding peace.

Sader sat down on a bench covered by a foam rubber cushion done in red velvet. He knew little of decorating but one glance told him that this was a professional job, and done expertly. "Your name was given us by Mrs. Champlain's former landlord. He thought you might know where she is now."

"She's dead." Wanda Nevins was sitting on another bench, not very near; she was lighting a cigarette from a copper-colored table lighter. "She's been dead for over six months."

"Can you tell me about it?"

"She went to Catalina with a pair of idiots. They owned a little outboard cruiser. They were swimming in one of the coves over there and she got cramps and went down and they let her drown. Her body was never recovered."

"Who were these people?"

She tapped the cigarette into the edge of the bowl where the little dwarf pine spread its green needles. "Do you mind answering a question or two, Mr. Sader? Just where is your office and who are these attorneys you represent?"

"My office is in Long Beach. You can find the address in the phone book. I can't give you the names of my clients, Miss Nevins. They have to guard against being approached by false heirs. I guess you might understand that."

"How much money is involved?" She studied his expression and shrugged. "Of course you wouldn't tell me that either. These people who let Tina drown at Catalina were friends of hers, a father and son. She was sort of interested in the son—of course you know that she was a widow."

"Yes, I know that."

"She had gone with Brent for about a year. He and the old man had built the boat. They were supposed to be pretty good sailors, knew their way on the channel. Of course that didn't have anything to do with her getting drowned."

"Who took her little boy? Who has him now?"

Sader's every instinct told him it wouldn't be this easy, and he was right. She smoked, looking at him across the glowing end of the cigarette. He thought that a little smile tugged at the corners of her mouth. "I have a hunch about you," she told him finally.

"And what is that?"

"It's the little boy you're after, really, isn't it?"

Sader wondered where he'd slipped. "Well, since the mother is dead, yes. We'd naturally want to find the child."

"He wasn't really Tina Champlain's child. He had been adopted. Now, you're going to have to tell me this much or this interview is closed. Is the money coming to the boy through Tina, or has it something to do with his real people?"

For some reason, Sader felt that the question was a trap. There was a way here in which he could ruin himself, though he didn't see it. On the other hand, she might really believe the yarn about the inheritance. Probably she'd automatically be interested where money was concerned. He made a bet with himself: she intended to deal herself in on this imaginary loot. "We had presumed that the boy was Mrs. Champlain's own baby," he said, feeling his way, "but I guess if there was nothing out of line about the way she got him—"

She had turned so that she no longer quite faced him, but faced the big Buddha on his pedestal. "You must mean that the money is coming through Tina Champlain. I didn't know that the family had any."

"You know them?"

"I've met some of her relatives."

"Just how well did you know Mrs. Champlain?"

"Pretty well. I don't mind confessing how I came to be as close to her as I was. You see, when I was a kid I had a rough time. My mother drank and my dad was gone all the time, and I ran away, and the cops got interested and then I was all tangled up with Juvenile Hall. They were getting ready to shove me into reform school, only Mrs. Champlain belonged to this Big Sister thing—that wasn't its name but it's the idea—and she stood good for my parole and got me straightened around. This was a long time before she found the . . . the baby she adopted."

"This little boy. . . ." Again Sader had the feeling that a false step would trap him in an error. "How did she find him? Through a recognized agency?"

"Oh, I helped her find him." Suddenly she got up off the teakwood bench and went over to stand beside the Buddha, looking out through the window at the sea. At this moment Sader heard a whining from outside, a scratching at the door, and remembered Gibbings saying that she owned a couple of boxer dogs. "Go away, Bruce." The scratching and whining died. "I'm talking too much, Mr. Sader. You have a way with you, a way of prying things out of people."

Not out of you I don't, Sader told himself. This was an act. She wanted time to think, or she figured he was on the hook and she wanted to play him a little.

"All of these things I've told you are confidential and personal. They might be used to hurt me, or others. I shouldn't have mentioned the fact that the boy was adopted." She paused here as if she expected him to say something. *What?* She went on, "That really is none of your business, since for all practical purposes an adoption is the same as a natural birth."

"That's right."

"Unless the person who has left this money to Tina's child has fixed it so that an adopted baby would be left out."

26

She was searching for a wedge, a way in; for something to trade. Sader decided to give her a little room. "I'd have to check that angle. It's possible, I suppose."

"If he were . . . illegitimate, for instance."

Sader said, "There are a lot of narrow-minded people in the world."

"But you wouldn't have to reveal it, would you? Aren't detectives allowed some choice about what is passed on to a client?"

He could see what was coming, now. They were going to end up as co-conspirators. He looked at her silhouette against the shoji screen and decided that he couldn't have found a prettier conspirator anywhere. Her torso in the brown sun suit had all the classic curves in the right places. The black curls shone like satin. "I'll have to talk it over with the attorneys. Then I'll know just what chances the baby has under the will." She didn't glance at him but he sensed her taut attention. "I'd just like to see him, make sure of the identity, if you know where he is now."

"I'm not trying to give you the run-around, Mr. Sader, but only some assurance that the baby is due to get the money would make me tell you where he is."

The tone was half-mocking, and he wondered if he'd really fooled her.

"This is what I'll do," she said. She turned. The big Buddha beside her lent her something foreign and enigmatic, a touch of mystery. "I'll check up on the little boy and make sure he's all right, that you'll be able to see him when the terms of the inheritance are cleared up. You can be checking with your clients."

"Good enough." Sader rose because he knew he wasn't going to find out from her where Gibbings' grandson was being kept . . . and perhaps abused.

"Let's try to get it for him," she said, walking forward. She moved softly but she didn't get very close. She was something you looked at but didn't touch. "Let's do all we can for the baby."

Her mind was on the money and she knew he knew it. The kid was a kind of humorist, Sader thought, knowing that he was up against a cunning and devious opponent.

CHAPTER THREE

Sader had a friend who worked the sports desk on the local paper. He got a pass from him to the newspaper morgue and looked up the account of the accident at Catalina in which Mrs. Champlain had died. The item was brief, and there had been apparently no follow-up, since the body had not been recovered. The owners of the boat were given as Ralph Perrine and his son, Brent. The address mentioned was in Wilmington.

It was getting along toward five o'clock now, dinner-time, and Sader decided he might have a good chance of finding the Perrines at home. At a quarter of six he pulled up in front of the house, a big old-fashioned frame place with a neglected yard. Out back were the unfinished hulls of three boats, the clutter of an amateur boatyard. Sader parked and got out, tested the gate. It started to fall loose, and he caught it and propped it against the fence post; the hinge was rusted to uselessness and he judged that this was the common procedure on entering. He went up the broken walk to the porch. He didn't have to knock. A tall man in shirt sleeves and work pants, gray-headed, stood inside the screen picking his teeth.

"Mr. Perrine?"

"Speaking."

Sader took out the I.D. and flashed it without any preliminary remarks. The man inside the screen door grunted. "We're looking for a Mrs. Champlain and her son."

The air seemed to stiffen up, Sader thought. The other man opened the screen and tossed the toothpick out, and thereby had a better look at Sader. "She's dead. I don't know where the kid is."

"Do you mind if I ask a few questions?"

"What about?"

"The relatives who might have taken the baby after her death."

He had pale gray eyes and they shone at Sader through the screen, and made Sader think of polished stones set in the tanned face. Perrine hesitated, not wanting Sader to come in. "Guess you'd better talk to my son. He knew her better'n I did." He opened the screen and came out. He was husky in spite of being stooped, with big gnarled hands, and Sader decided that he was a man who had worked hard all his life. "My son's out back. Come on." He trotted down the steps, the porch shuddering, and turned at the side of the house toward the clutter at the rear.

The smell of paint and of wood shavings was powerful. The man who turned to look at them was one of the best examples of the outdoor type Sader had ever seen. He was big. He wore a frayed T shirt and tight denims, and he filled them to muscular perfection. The face was square and masculine, the eyebrows dark and heavy, the hair crewcut over his well-shaped head, and he examined Sader with intelligent attention while his father explained that Sader wanted information about Mrs. Champlain's adopted boy.

"Are you a cop, Mr. Sader?" he asked quietly.

"I'm a private investigator."

"And who're you working for?"

"A bunch of lawyers," Sader said, trotting out the convenient half-truth. "There's some money, an inheritance, involved. We didn't know that Mrs. Champlain is dead; but since it's true, we'd like to locate the boy."

He thought that he saw a flash of suspicion in Brent's face, but if there had been, Brent covered it quickly. He laid down his paintbrush, took a pack of cigarettes from his pocket, then hesitated before lighting one. "Let's get away from the paint. I'm always afraid of fire out here." He moved perhaps a dozen feet, turned around, lighted the cigarette and inhaled the smoke. "After Tina died I lost contact with the people we'd known together. Anyway, I scarcely knew her relatives. I'd met a couple of aunts. An uncle once."

"Were they her relatives, or relatives of her dead husband?"

"I never heard her mention anyone in her husband's family. These people were her own relatives."

Mentally Sader filed it into the same category with something else he had already figured out: Gibbings would have investigated, on his own, anyone listed under the name of Champlain in the city directories or the phone books. The boy wouldn't be with any of them. "Do you remember their names?"

Brent went on puffing at the cigarette, and looking thoughtful, and finally he said, "I've got a letter in the house, one that Tina wrote me. There's something in it about one of the aunts. Let's go have a look." He turned, walked past the jutting prow of an unfinished hull and headed for the rear door of the house, with the old man still mumbling a protest because he didn't want Sader to get indoors. Sader moved along hurriedly.

Since the day was dying outdoors, the house was dark. Brent snapped on the lights. The kitchen looked like the tail end of a wrecking party. There was a table covered with beer cans and chicken bones, curling rinds of pizzas and a snowflake pile where somebody had peeled some boiled eggs. The sink had dishes in it—not stacked; they looked as if they had been aimed at the sink from across the room. Mixed with china and pots were paper plates and wadded napkins. The chairs held stacks of old newspapers, with soiled shirts and other washables draped over their backs. Brent waved at it all in passing. "Don't mind this. We don't have time to keep house."

The old man whined louder, and Sader judged that this was what he wasn't supposed to see. In the hall, Brent snapped on more lights and said, "Wait down here, I'll find the letter and be right back," and ran up the stairs to the second floor. The old man went on into another room, switched on a lamp. Sader could see the end of a scuffy green rug and a chair. The cushion in the chair had stuffing escaping, which was par for the course, Sader thought.

The old man was grumbling in there, and Sader caught fragments about nosy interlopers, and why couldn't people be allowed to keep their privacy.

He heard Brent on the stairs and turned. Brent had stopped on the landing where the stairs turned. He had an open letter in his hand. He moved the sheets of paper so that light fell on them from the upper hall, and read what was written. Then reread the page. He lowered the sheets and looked at Sader. Sader thought Brent wore an odd expression. He seemed jolted, stunned. Puzzled, too. All at once Sader's uneasy intuition told him he wasn't going to see that letter, and the apprehension and anger dried his mouth and throat. He swallowed. He wanted to go up after Brent Perrine, but that wouldn't be any good. Brent had about twenty years on him, not to mention all that muscle. Sader stayed put and waited.

He tried to sound casual. "Well, what's it say?"

Brent didn't come down any farther. He rubbed a free hand over his crewcut. He was shielding his eyes, but Sader could sense the air of surprise and of unbelief. Then Brent said, "Hell, this isn't the right letter. I've made a mistake." He turned quickly and with a gesture of tucking the letter out of Sader's sight, he ran back up the stairs. When he didn't come back in a couple of minutes, Sader went on into the living room.

Ralph Perrine was taking a bottle of wine from under the lid of a phonograph cabinet. He frowned at Sader.

"Go ahead," Sader said, "don't mind me."

Perrine tilted the quart of muscatel and took a lingering drink.

Sader sat on the edge of the wrecked chair. "I understand that Mrs. Champlain was swimming off your boat when she was drowned."

Perrine wiped his mouth with the back of his hand. He returned the muscatel to the cabinet, closed the lid. He seemed suddenly gloomy. "That's right, mister. It was a terrible thing, too. She was a young and pretty woman and she was sure sweet on my boy. I know Brent was fond of her, too. I was hoping they'd get married. She could of helped him, she could of bought a place where he could have his own boatyard, his own business. It just ruined it all, her drowning like that."

"What do you mean, she could have helped him?"

"She had all that money from her husband's death. The insurance." Perrine spoke as if Sader in his stupidity must have forgotten. "He had the regular life insurance, and then he took out some of that flight insurance before the plane took off. She was a rich woman, though you wouldn't think it. She didn't have no airs about her. I liked her for that."

Sader flinched. As soon as Gibbings had mentioned that Champlain had died on a flight, he should have thought of insurance.

"Who has the money now?"

"The child, I guess. Wouldn't he inherit it?"

Brother, brother. I really ought to have my head examined, Sader thought in anger. He listened for sounds of Brent's coming down again, and heard nothing, and knew that Brent was up there with the letter, rereading that page of it, as clearly as if he had seen it.

He thought of Gibbings. What kind of game was the old fox playing, pretending he didn't want to reclaim the grandson now worth a fortune? "Did Mrs. Champlain ever say anything to you about making a will?"

"Sure did." Perrine sidled back to the old phonograph and his fingers twiddled on the lid. "She talked about it a lot. She was going to leave half of her money to Brent. Not that she thought anything would happen to her. None of us dreamed anything like that. I guess . . ." He yanked up the lid as if expecting Sader to make a protest. "I guess she forgot. Or she really meant to do it when they got married."

Sader watched while Perrine had another go at the muscatel. "How much of a search did you make for her body?"

"We spent a week," Perrine said promptly. "Brent just about didn't get over it. I thought he'd get drowned hisself, he spent so much time in the water. She never came up, and he couldn't find her."

"Anybody help?"

"Plenty. Skin divers, the Coast Guard, a lot of the people who had boats at Catalina—they all hunted for her."

"What time of day was it? Was she swimming alone?"

"We went over the night before, and Brent and I fished, and then he took her ashore to a hotel in Avalon. Next day we took out about noon. She and Brent were in the water and I was fishing when it happened. She just gave a kind of yell and went under. Just like that." He snapped his gnarled fingers.

"The water at Catalina is pretty clear. It's a wonder you didn't see her on the bottom."

"We were out in deep water. I used to wonder if it hadn't been a shark got her. A million-to-one chance, according to those fellas who know all about fishes, but still—"

"If a shark got her, you'd have seen the blood."

"Guess that's right."

Sader tried to analyze the old man's attitude, but on the surface he seemed genuinely puzzled and unhappy about what had happened to Tina Champlain.

"It was early in the spring. Early for swimming, I mean."

"It sure was," Perrine agreed. "I remember Brent complaining. She didn't mind the cold as much. I've noticed it before—women don't."

Sader heard a sound from the hall and looked around. Brent Perrine was standing in the doorway. He looked directly at Sader, a kind of look that Sader recognized—he was covering a lie with a stare—and said, "Well, that's the limit. I can't find that letter up there anywhere."

"Too bad. You don't remember the aunt's name?"

"It was Sawyer, or something like it. Sawnell. No, that's not it."

"Do you think she might have taken Mrs. Champlain's little boy, after she was drowned?"

"I don't know. It's possible, though this aunt was pretty well along in years. She was Mrs. Champlain's father's sister, his oldest sister. I remember that much."

"What about the uncle you met?"

Brent shrugged. He had his eye on the lid of the phonograph, and old man Perrine was across the room from it, very innocent. Sader suddenly got the picture of what went on here, the young man holding down a job and trying in his spare time to make a start in the boat business, and the old man supposed to help by keeping the house going, and instead hitting the bottle. Brent had ambition and energy. The old man was burned out.

"I don't remember the uncle's name. I don't even remember if she mentioned it. I think she just said, 'This is my Uncle Joe,' or something like that. He was a tall old guy. A nice dresser. That's all I remember about him."

"These people live around here? Near L.A.?"

"I think they do."

"What about mutual friends? Someone you knew while you and Tina Champlain were going together?"

He had the feeling that Brent was withdrawing from these questions, that there was a secret he meant to guard. He wondered if it had something to do with that letter. Brent said, "There was one couple—they lived in West L.A. They were neighbors of hers at the time she'd been married to Champlain. But they moved East, I don't know where."

"What about a girl named Wanda Nevins?"

It startled Brent. He hadn't expected it. He made a couple of false starts and then said, "She was a friend of Tina's. I met her a couple of times. She was younger than Tina, Tina had helped her out of some kind of jam. I don't think Tina saw much of her. It was just . . . old acquaintance."

"Have you seen her since Mrs. Champlain's death?"

Brent hesitated, the awkward moment drawing out while he decided what to say about Wanda Nevins. "She came here once. She thought Tina might have left her some money, and she wanted to know what we knew about a will. We didn't know anything. I don't think Tina made one. I told her that, and she left, and I haven't seen her since."

Sader made one last try. "Can you think of anything—anything at all—which might give a clue as to who has Mrs. Champlain's little boy?"

Brent and his father exchanged a glance. As far as Sader could tell they seemed honestly puzzled by the question. "I just don't know," Brent said at last. "When she went out with me she had a baby sitter come in. An older woman, a neighbor. But as for who'd have him now . . . I really just don't know."

Sader drove down to Fisherman's Wharf for a sea-food dinner. He had coffee first, trying to rouse himself from a sour feeling of let-down. The restaurant was clean and brightly lighted, smelled appetizingly of food, and from below the windows the moving surf gurgled around the pilings. It was pleasant, even sort of romantic, but nothing lifted his mood.

He thought back through the day, wondering what he might have done differently. He'd had a nice trip down the coast to Laguna, an interesting sidelight on running a boatyard at home. The one thing he had learned which might make a difference, was that there was a lot of money involved. Gibbings hadn't mentioned it, and he wanted to tell Gibbings while he could watch him.

There was something inside the amorphous case, a hard core he couldn't quite get a grip on. He tried to think of a comparison and remembered something his grandmother had said once, something about a flatiron inside a feather bed. There was a flatiron somewhere inside this thing but he couldn't find it. He just knew that it was there. A booby trap.

The waitress came with the fried shrimp and the Idaho baked potato and the creamed peas, and Sader picked up his fork, and then suddenly he remembered something out of the letter Gibbings had showed him, something about the child going hungry, half-starved. He laid down the fork.

The blonde came tripping back with a small plate containing two fat chunks of hot corn bread, two pats of butter and strawberry jam. "Would you like your coffee warmed up, sir?"

"No, thanks."

He began to eat, because not to would look silly and anyway it had to be paid for, but the zest was gone.

Somewhere not too far away, somewhere in the coastal triangle, say between here and Santa Monica and draw the line east to Santa Anita track and back to the beach, somewhere in that chunk of city was a small child who was living a life of hell.

He managed two and a half shrimps, and one chunk of corn bread, and had a final cup of coffee, black. Then he went back to the car.

The night smelled of the sea. Out in the dark some ships rode at anchor. One of them must be Navy. A blinker began to wink against the dark, sending God knew what kind of important information, maybe, Sader thought, something about the admiral's girl friend being late for their date and if she didn't hurry he'd have to go on home to his wife.

It was against Sader's principles to work at night.

He headed for the office.

CHAPTER FOUR

Sader knew one attorney with an insane habit of staying downtown nights to practice putting in his empty office. Sader rang him.

He was hard to pin down as any lawyer is, talking back to Sader's questions under a cloud of quibbling phrases, but in the end Sader got answers, of sorts. The lawyer also promised to check with somebody in the new L.A. County Courthouse and see if Mrs. Champlain's will had been filed or steps taken to probate her estate. Six months was early for such action, he warned. The courts were crowded.

Since Mrs. Champlain legally had disappeared rather than died, he pointed out, her property might have been put into trusteeship. The property of missing persons was kept in trusteeship for seven years unless the person returned or was found dead. However, the court would listen to evidence of a presumed death, such as being lost off a boat. He made this sound as curious as though it had never happened before, then admitted to Sader that he was presently at work trying to settle the estate of a client who had fallen overboard into the Catalina Channel.

"With all the boats we have hereabouts, it must happen all the time," Sader insisted.

"Well, yes, unfortunately people don't seem to keep their minds on what they are doing."

"Suppose this woman didn't leave a will? What about the adopted baby, the other relatives?"

"Legally the baby should get most of it. The relatives can put in a claim, of course. Or they can contest a will. You've got a very involved affair there, Sader. All sorts of complicated possibilities. Did the baby for instance inherit directly any part of that flight insurance?"

"I don't know. I guess it would be a hell of a job to find out."

"You see? That's just one angle. Whereas . . ." He was off again. Sader waited for a break and then asked, "How much of a job is it to cancel an adoption?"

"For what cause?"

"Death of the adoptive parents."

"Death doesn't cancel the adoption, Sader. The child is considered the heir, he hasn't been returned to the original parents by the fact of losing the new ones. Do you want me to write you a legal opinion?"

"I'll let you know."

"I'd have to do a lot of reading even to venture an opinion. You've got a complicated snarl there, legally."

"Yes, you said so. Thanks a lot anyway."

"Perhaps Mrs. Champlain left the money in trust."

It could be, Sader thought. She might have put it in trust right after the husband's death, too; she didn't seem to have spent much of it to judge by the neighborhood she'd lived in. Maybe she played the horses or something, though. As his friend had mentioned, there were a lot of possibilities. "If you can find out whether the will has been filed, I'd appreciate it."

"Will do."

"Don't crack any windows."

"What?"

"With a wild putt."

"Oh. Ha, ha."

Sader put the phone in its cradle and picked up his cigarette from the ash tray.

While he sat thinking, the night quiet was broken by a sudden gust and spatter at the windows. It had begun to rain. He sat watching the panes, faintly illumined by lights in the street below, covered now by a silvery sparkle. When the cigarette was done he got up, put on his coat and hat again, locked the office and went back to the car. He drove north on Pine Avenue, looking for a certain bar. The streets were practically deserted, the evening strollers driven indoors by the shower. When he found the bar, he parked and went in, and saw his friend of the sports desk sitting there with a couple of cronies, other reporters. Sader got him into a booth off to the side, and ordered a couple of drinks.

"I know you're acquainted with a lot of L.A. newspaper people," Sader said, while they waited. "I need an introduction to somebody on a society page. Some woman with sense who won't be afraid to give out with some frank information."

His friend, whose name was Berryman, thought about it. "She's got to be working at it?"

"What do you mean?"

"I know an old gal who retired a couple of years ago. She knows more dirt than anybody, anywhere. I'm taking for granted it's dirt that you're after." The waitress brought their drinks. Berryman took a suspicious look at the tall one she set in front of Sader. "What's that?"

"Soda and lemon."

"You're still on the wagon?"

"I don't have much choice."

"You really can't stop, once you get started?"

"So I've discovered." Sader picked up the drink and tasted it. "Can we call this woman now?"

"You mean, on the phone? Why bother? She lives less than a dozen blocks from here. Crazy about the beach and the Pike. She moved down here, I think to play bingo. She's good for a drink, too. In fact she's kind of insistent, so brace yourself." Berryman picked up the shot, neat, and threw it past his tonsils and chased it with a swallow of water. "Come on." He got up and walked out, slapping the backs of his friends in passing. "I'll see you later, buddies." Outside he stretched his arms and looked at the sky. "My God, it's raining!"

"You miss a lot of weather, staying in there," Sader pointed out. He got in behind the wheel, Berryman getting in at the other door. "Tell me where to go."

They drove south toward the beach, down the incline of

the bluff, then crept through a wet alley where old apartments showed their backsides, the clotheslines and the stacked boxes of trash. "Yeah, here it is."

Sader drew into a parking space and set the brakes. It was an old two-storey court, a double row of apartments facing each other across a paved slot. There were puddles of rain water around some potted geraniums out in the middle. Berryman paused at a door to knock.

When she opened the door, Sader saw an elephant of a woman in tight red pants, green jersey blouse, ropes of junk jewelry, and Japanese thong sandals. She was chewing gum. She wore a lot of rouge and mascara. She was nothing at all like Sader's idea of a society reporter. He'd met a few in his day and they'd all been ladylike ladies in trim suits and white gloves, very conscious of their good manners. This one looked as if she must have retired from a circus.

She looked at Berryman and cried, "Why, you raunchy bastard, what are you doing down here at this hour?"

"I've pleaded and begged," Berryman said smirking, "and I've tried every trick in the book, and now my patience is gone. I'm going to rape you."

She opened her mouth to squeal, showing a lot of big white teeth. "Out here on the porch? Where people can see us? You'll get me kicked out!"

"The landlord must have passed up a thousand opportunities before now."

She was looking at Sader. "Say . . . Quit your horsing around and introduce me to your friend. He's cute." She patted her platinum hair.

"This is Sader, Betty. He's a private eye and he wants to meet you."

"Me? What've I done?" She moved back in pretended alarm, and they went in. "Is this on the level? Are you really a private detective?"

Sader said yes, that's what he was. He was sizing up the place. She must have been spending a lot of time on the Pike because the place had all kinds of plaster dolls and toys, satin pillows, and other trinkets offered as prizes. He thought it all looked junky but homey. She made him and Berryman sit down, and brought them drinks. Sader put his drink on the table by his elbow; when the right time came he'd exchange it for Berryman's empty glass. Berryman was explaining that Sader wanted some inside information, probably for blackmail purposes.

"I don't know much about the doings in the hinterlands, like Long Beach," she explained. "I always worked in L.A."

"This concerns people in L.A. I wondered what you could tell me about a woman named Kit Gibbings."

For a moment her face was blank, and then she looked incredulous. "You don't mean . . . not the daughter of old Hale Gibbings?"

"Yes, that's the one."

"Katharyn Gibbings?" She frowned at him, and he saw that the frolicsome mood was vanishing. "Nobody ever called her Kit that I knew of. Unless it might have been the old man. What do you want to know about her?"

"Just whatever you can tell me. The kind of person she is. Where she lives now. How well you knew her, anything."

She sat looking at him with what Sader thought was a curious hostility. "You've never met her?"

"No."

"Met the old man?"

"Yes."

"She's not a bit like him. When I was acting like a lady myself, before I moved down here and went to the dogs, I used to think that Katharyn Gibbings was the most perfect example of a gentlewoman I'd ever known. I haven't seen her for years . . . six, maybe seven years. The last time I saw her was at the races. Hollywood Park. She was in the clubhouse sitting alone at a table, studying the racing form."

"She liked to gamble?"

"She went to the track on Charity Days. I never saw her there any other times."

"How does it happen you haven't seen her for so long?"

"She dropped out of things. All at once. Just quit going anywhere. She must have been sick for a while. People asked about her—not a lot of them, she was a quiet woman, she didn't have any style and there was never any scandal about her. I don't think she had many friends. She served on a few committees, did volunteer work at the hospitals, that kind of doings."

"And this particular day, the day at Hollywood Park? What about that?"

"I guess I remembered it because something kind of hit me. I'd been drinking a little, and I got to looking around at the people . . . and well, you know how it is when you're

about half-whacked and suddenly you become very phil-
osophical? Or maybe I mean psychological. Anyway, you
get a sort of terrific insight. You suddenly see everybody
very clearly and you sum up their lives and their person-
alities to yourself, like a camera shutter going *click*? And
there's a horrible finality about it?"

"God, do I know what you mean!" Berryman groaned.

"So do I," said Sader.

"Well, I was sitting there peering about in this unfo-
cused way and I saw Katharyn Gibbings at a table, reading the racing form as if she knew what it was all about.
She had a pot of tea, a cup poured for herself, her white
kid gloves lying there by the saucer and a nice white handbag. She was wearing a brown linen suit and a brown hat.
The hat was utterly nothing. She'd paid fifty dollars for it
somewhere and they'd robbed her. The suit was nice but
it wasn't good for her." Betty was sitting under a lamp, the
glow shining in her platinum hair and the myriad strands
of beads around her neck. She moved restlessly as if the
memory still annoyed her. "And all at once while I looked
at her, just like *that*"—Betty snapped her fingers sharply—
"it came over me what kind of life she lived. Stuffy. Cooped
up. Being old man Gibbings' daughter. Shut up in that
white mausoleum in Tiffany Square. For that matter, shut
up in Tiffany Square and only knowing the other fossils
that lived in it. Pushing forty, turning gray. Little lines in
her lips. Minding her manners and pretending she didn't
care. And worst of all, having nothing at all in her that
would lead her to revolt. She was *gentle* . . . so godaw-
ful and everlastingly *gentle*. A soft, sweet, pudding pie of

a woman. I'll tell you, Mr. Private Eye Sader, if there's one woman in L.A. you'll never dig up any dirt about, it's Katharyn Gibbings." She slapped a hand on the thigh of the red pants and nodded emphatically.

"But you haven't seen her for years," Sader pointed out.

"I know her. She wouldn't change. My God, I've known her for twenty-five years. She was a kid, she was going to Miss What's-her-name's school, the one on West Adams that burned down. I was just starting in as a society reporter. They were teaching me not to spill tea on myself and how to keep from insulting that old dragon, the wife of the man who owned the opposition paper and ran all the charity rackets. I remember Katharyn Gibbings from that first year. She was a sort of cute child, and then her eyes went bad on her and she had to wear glasses. She was the kind of girl who looked homely in them. I don't think she ever had a beau. Hey, you aren't drinking that drink I made you!"

"Give me time, I'll get to it."

Betty got up and went to the kitchen, came back with a bottle of whiskey and freshened the drink. "There. Ice has melted, that'll take up the slack." She took the whiskey over to her own drink and put in a dollop. "What I was going to add, though—I think that day at the races, and seeing Katharyn Gibbings and thinking what I did about her, was what made me what I am today. I just suddenly wanted to do a lot of crazy things. Kind of in protest, I guess."

"Baby, you're wonderful," Berryman told her. "I can't imagine you drinking tea and being nice to a dragon."

"I'd go into L.A. and give her a kick in the ass today,"

Betty said, "only meanwhile it happens she has died. She was a bitch. She treated us like dogs because we worked for a union paper and her husband was a labor baiter." Betty downed about half of the drink. "But getting back to Katharyn Gibbings . . . I guess I've told you about everything I know. She's a nice, sweet woman—wherever she is."

"What about Katharyn's mother, Gibbings' wife?" Sader asked.

She bared her big white teeth. "Personally I could never quite believe he'd had one, the old tyrant. But I guess he did. There was Katharyn, and other people had known the mother, from all reports an utterly humble and colorless woman who died when Katharyn was a kid. Poor kid!"

"You don't like him much?"

"Gibbings? Since you know him—"

"I met him briefly."

"What was it you really wanted to know about Katharyn Gibbings?"

Sader saw the suspicion in her eyes. "Just what you've told me."

"Really? Was that all?" She downed the rest of her drink and looked pointedly at the one by Sader's elbow. Berryman caught the glance. He held his own empty glass out toward her. "How about a refill, baby?" When she was gone, he grabbed Sader's glass and took it down by half.

"My God," Sader said.

"I'm doing you a favor, man!"

"I guess you are, at that."

"What's with the Gibbings woman?" Berryman asked, openly curious.

"Just an angle concerning a case I'm working on."

"She sounds like the original virgin spinster."

"She sure does," Sader agreed.

"Unless, of course," Berryman said, taking the drink down again, "she started kicking up her heels after Betty lost track of her."

"That doesn't seem likely."

"You let the ice melt and this is weak as hell!"

Betty came back with Berryman's fresh drink, noted approvingly the glass now empty by Sader's side. The conversation turned to newspaper shoptalk. Betty knew a lot of gossip, and her comments on some of her and Berryman's mutual acquaintances sent Berryman into stitches. Sader smiled over her caustic wit, but inwardly he was thinking about Katharyn Gibbings.

He had probed here into territory which old man Gibbings had forbidden him, satisfying his own curiosity. The kind of woman Katharyn was could have no relation to where her child was now and what was happening to him, but it seemed to Sader that he had needed to know, needed to fill in that blank part of the picture.

However clever Betty was, however shrewd her insight in that moment of illumination, she had missed the truth about Katharyn Gibbings. The woman sitting alone at the table in the Hollywood Park clubhouse had been on the verge of explosive rebellion. She had been about to trade her repressed virginity for unlawful motherhood. Sader couldn't help wondering what Katharyn Gibbings thought of the exchange by now.

CHAPTER FIVE

Sader dropped Berryman at the bar and returned to his office.

It was late now. The cleaning women had done their job and departed, the building was dark. He turned on lights in the inner office and sat down at the desk, took out some blank sheets and began to write up the day's work, omitting of course the last hour or so, the visit with Betty. If Gibbings found it in a report he'd blow his stack.

Sader glanced at the clock, jotting the time at the bottom of the page: 11:29. He slipped the paper into an upper drawer, was closing the desk, when he heard a sound in the outer office. His head lifted and he waited. The sound came again, a step. Then Wanda Nevins came in, blinking at the light. She wasn't in scanty garb this time, but her figure was as good as ever. She had on a tan wool dress and a little black fur jacket. There was a frosting of raindrops on her hair. Her lipstick was the color of firecrackers. Behind her moved something big and tawny, a giant of a dog.

The dog examined Sader as if Sader might be made of beefsteak.

"What a trip! Just wet enough to skid on!" She came closer to the desk, but not close enough to touch. She smiled and brushed the Persian lamb jacket off her shoulders.

"I thought maybe you rode the animal from Laguna. He's big enough to saddle."

A slim hand dropped to touch the tawny ears. "Oh, Bruce is just a baby, a puppy."

"I'd hate to meet him when he's grown."

She smiled again, lazily. Sader thought she seemed very sure of herself, covering some inner jubilation, a kind of smugness, and he wondered what she had been up to since he had seen her at home. After Sader offered a chair, and she sat down, she said mockingly, "You tickled my curiosity today. I know that you detectives have to keep secrets —but you were so *damned* mysterious!"

"Really? I didn't mean to be," Sader said. She had taken cigarettes from her handbag, selected one from the pack. She gave him a swift, measuring glance over the light he held for her. Sader went on, "How did you happen to drop in now? After all, even detectives are supposed to sleep nights."

"If you hadn't been here, I was going to get in somehow and prowl your office."

"I don't doubt it."

She edged back to the subject she'd chosen. "I've been thinking about Tina's little boy. I suppose you know who he really is? I mean, who he belonged to before Tina got him?"

Sader smiled a little. "That doesn't carry any weight in this affair."

"You just want to be satisfied that he was legally adopted by the Champlains?"

"Mostly, yes. And find him." Sader was trying to pin down his impression that she had a secret, a hole card, something she had learned this afternoon. Her manner simmered with excitement; there was color in her face. Even the big dog lying at her feet looked perked-up, alert. "The main thing is to locate him and see him, make sure he's all right." Their eyes met for a moment. Hers seemed to dance. "If I remember rightly, you hinted today that Tina Champlain found the child through you. The mother was someone you had known during that time you were in trouble."

Her bright mouth puckered with an appearance of dismay. "Oh, dear, did I let that drop?"

"Yes, you did."

"People trusted me. I have to be careful."

Sader said patiently, "You want the child to be well cared for, don't you?"

"Of course. It's because of him that I need to watch every word I say."

Sader was suddenly tired of her game. She wanted to lead him by the nose to some prearranged surprise, some point of revelation, where he would stand flat-footed and at a loss while she crowed over her advantage. "I think you're worrying over nothing," he said. "We aren't interested in the past, the child's original background. It's the present that counts. I want to see him. That's all."

54

Her face stiffened. "You said it concerned money. An inheritance."

Sader shrugged, waited. He remembered how she had stood looking at him from beside the big Buddha, his impression then that he would never get anything from her. And with dry amusement he realized how she would have affected old man Gibbings.

"You said that the situation might change if the baby had been illegitimate."

"I talked to the lawyers," Sader said, "and they said not to worry. Just to find the kid. Why don't you tell me where he is?"

She had come in primed to play a game, and Sader hadn't responded. He saw from the studying look in her eye that she was in search of a new approach. "I don't know where the little boy is now." The dog cocked his head as if something in his mistress's voice puzzled him—perhaps the effort to sound honest. "I tried to find out today. Not exactly just to tell you, because I don't know yet whose side you're on."

"Just say I'm on the kid's side."

She crushed out the cigarette. "You can joke about it, Mr. Sader, but believe me, if you're ignorant of the baby's real background you've been short-changed. I know that none of Tina's people ever had a dime. Do you know what her father does for a living? He's a railroad station agent, a little place in eastern Canada."

Sader was watching her. "He's still alive?"

"As of four o'clock this afternoon. I talked to him by phone, and he never heard of any money coming to Tina or the baby . . . nothing that wasn't collected at the time of that plane crash, when Champlain was killed." By the flush of color in her face, the lift of her chin, Sader knew that this was part of it, part of the secret; and he sensed that she had parted with this much to lead him on again. "We can be honest with each other, can't we? You can admit, for instance, that the people who want to find the baby don't want to give him any money. They want *him*."

Sader shook his head. "You're wrong. There's no intention of claiming the child again. You know the mother. You know—let's put it this way—the person who handled all the details of the adoption. He hasn't changed, and he won't." Sader remembered Gibbings' warning, that he was not in any case to be identified as the baby's grandfather. This was the time to remember that warning. "There's nothing you can sell him. There is something you can sell me. For one hundred dollars. The name of the relative who has Tina Champlain's child."

Sader opened the right-hand drawer and took out the office checkbook and opened it in front of him. Wanda Nevins had risen from her chair. Sader looked up at her, wondering at her silence. He thought that she seemed shocked, that there was a sudden pallor in her face.

"Are you selling?" he said.

She stared at him as if not understanding. He tapped the checkbook with the tip of his pen. "One hundred. Pocket money. Might buy next month's nylons."

"I'll have to think about it." She was moving away. The big dog got to his feet with a grunt, padded after her, his toenails tapping the floor. She stopped at the door to the outer room, and Sader decided this was the point at which he was supposed to up the ante. He grinned to himself. When she glanced back at him he pretended to cover a yawn. She snapped a finger at Bruce, and went on into the other room, and then her voice drifted back to him. "Believe me, Mr. Sader, you're working in the *dark*."

The door shut and Sader sat there with an elbow propped on the open checkbook. He waited for her to come back, and she didn't. After about ten minutes, he knew that she was gone. He'd never been so surprised in his life.

He woke up in the middle of the night and thought about it.

The unfamiliar house was big, echoing and yet silent —echoing *with* silence, Sader thought. He had agreed to move in and look after his partner's hunting dog, and Scarborough's aunt's parrot, during the time Scarborough would be in San Francisco and his aunt visiting in Salt Lake. This meant feeding the dog morning and night, refilling the bird's water cup and seed dish without getting his fingers bitten off, and listening for the jets from Los Alamitos to take off a chunk of chimney. The house was out in the country, sort of. There were tracts on three sides, where once had been orange groves. He was positive that Scarborough clung to the incongruous arrangement in hopes of inheriting his aunt's money. Scarborough was young, lively, and brash, always looking for kicks. His aunt was a small critical person who knitted afghans and hated cats. The fact that the house was so big and that they could live in it without running into each other too often must be a help, in Sader's opinion.

He found cigarettes, lighted one in the dark, got up from the guest-room bed and went to the window to smoke, looking through the misty night at the lights of Los Alamitos. The pane had raindrops on it, and when a jet went over low they vibrated glitteringly, and a dozen let go and slid down the glass. He thought about Wanda's parting remark, and let it circle around in his mind while he examined it. Something he had said to her had worked a change, and he couldn't imagine what it had been.

He smoked, and listened to the night. When the jets weren't going over, it was very quiet. He rubbed the back of his neck with his free hand, and found that he was tired without being sleepy, and that by trying not to think of the letter old man Gibbings had received he had brought it ferociously to life.

Say that it was true, and that somewhere out there in the night, right now, an abused child had found a few hours of peace in uneasy sleep.

What kind of person would treat a kid like that?

Somebody who hated kids, couldn't abide them, felt about them the way Scarborough's aunt felt about cats.

No.

He felt as if he had been yanked back from that mistake by physical force. The cigarette hung dry and tasteless from his lips, and his eyes burned as if he'd never get them shut again. He had been a fool, and far amiss in the heart of this matter. For the person who was abusing the child must be someone who had hated Tina Champlain with the fury of a million hells.

He saw the questions he should have asked, and felt a sour disgust for his lack of insight. He had indeed, as Wanda had said, been working in the dark.

He was clutched by a vast urge to haste, but there was nothing to be done now, in the middle of the night. He lighted a second cigarette off the first and forced himself to stand calm and to plan the day ahead.

The Lakeside Chapel of St. John's stood alone at the foot of a knoll, shaded by a clump of pepper trees and facing a small artificial lagoon full of water lilies. The chapel was mostly of glass, with redwood beams. Across the front, a great mural panel in mosaic tile portrayed the baptism of Christ. That took care, Sader thought, of any question about which St. John was meant. He parked at the curb and got out, crossing the velvet quarter-acre of lawn, sniffing the freshness of morning.

The chapel was locked, deserted, but a small brass plate tacked to the inner frame of the mural gave the minister's name and address. Sader followed the quiet street around to the other side of the knoll, to a neat white stucco cottage. When he rang the bell, a housekeeper in a blue-striped uniform came to the door.

"Is the reverend in?"

"Mr. Twining had to go out early on sick call," she said. She seemed very prim, and the uniform was full of starch. "May I help you?"

"Did you know a couple named Champlain, who used to attend church here?"

She thought it over for a minute. "They were young people. Mr. Champlain was killed in a plane crash. About two years ago, I think."

"Mrs. Champlain is dead, too. I'm trying to find any friends or neighbors, someone who knew them well when they lived out here."

She drew back, opening the door. "Won't you come in? Mr. Twining should be back pretty soon, and he may be able to find something for you in the church records." She ushered him into a small formal room. "What did you say your name was?"

"Sader. I'm a private investigator."

"I see." She seemed to take on a cautious air, as if private detectives might threaten the order of her starched existence. "Does it have something to do with Mrs. Champlain's death?"

Couldn't resist it, Sader thought, saying, "No, I'm trying to find her child. You said something about church records. If they'd had the baby baptized here, there would have been godparents."

"Yes, there would have been." She hesitated. "I don't remember a christening in connection with the Champlains, but there may have been one. We'll wait for Mr. Twining and then we'll know."

"Mr. Twining wasn't the minister here at the time, was he?"

"That was Dr. Bell."

She went out, leaving Sader on a maple bench. He

thought about smoking and then gave up the idea. This room had never been smoked in.

When Mr. Twining arrived, he proved to be a well-built young man in a tweedy suit and horn-rims, whose scholarly air overlaid a lot of energy. He offered Sader coffee, and broke out a pipe and filled it. He put the pipe between his teeth but didn't light it, and when he saw Sader looking at it, he said, "I smoke in my study only. On account of Mrs. Mimms."

"I can see how that would work out," Sader agreed.

The coffee Mrs. Mimms brought was fresh and hot. Mr. Twining stirred in sugar and said, "Now, let's see, you've come about the Champlains. I didn't know them; they were before my time. I took over this parish less than two years ago. Dr. Bell mentioned them a couple of times, while I was getting settled. He asked me to keep an eye on Mrs. Champlain and the baby. About a year ago he wrote me that he'd heard from Mrs. Champlain, and he enclosed an address, but when I found time—I was awfully busy about then—when I found time to look it up, the place had been condemned for some kind of freeway extension."

"I was there yesterday. The whole neighborhood's being wrecked and hauled away. There isn't anyone I can ask about the baby."

"Yes. The baby. Well, I'll have a look at the baptismal records. There may not be anything. You see, we're an interdenominational church. We take in a cross section of Protestant people, and among them are many who don't believe in infant baptism, and so we don't insist on it."

Sader felt a premonition, a lurching loss of confidence.

"Anything you can give me—"

"Yes. Well, I'll check and come back."

Sader waited another fifteen minutes. When Mr. Twining came in, one glance told Sader the errand had been fruitless. "There is no record of the baby's baptism, Mr. Sader. I'm sorry to have been so long, but I double-checked to be sure. The only thing I can offer is this. While Mrs. Champlain was a member of our church she attended some of the Women's Circle meetings. I know this because her name is on the rolls. I can give you the name and address of the chairman for that year."

"I'd appreciate that."

Mr. Twining wrote on a sheet of paper *Mrs. William Forrest, 22318 Silverbirch*, and told Sader how to find it.

Twenty minutes later, walking up the flagged path from the curb, Sader made a guess at how much Mr. Forrest had laid on the line for it, and decided that it hadn't been a cent under fifty thousand. It was a nice house, low and comfortably ranchy without being old-corral about it, not a mansion but as good as the rest of the neighborhood, which was pretty nice indeed. Sader noted the carriage lamp by the entry, the fall iris in bloom under the windows, big blue flags mixed with gold. The knocker was brass, a horse's head, very graceful.

The maid came and said that Mrs. Forrest wasn't at home. She was spending a week in Palm Springs.

Sader turned from the door. He hesitated there a moment. The street was winding, curving off westward between the wide green lawns and the big houses. It was a quiet street, an upper-class kind of street. There was no traffic, no kids running around loose, no stray bikes dropped down, no hollering, no grubby hopscotch or impromptu baseball; and Sader stood looking at it with a new expression in his eyes.

Tina Champlain had lived in this neighborhood until her husband had died in a plane crash. Then, though it would seem that she could have stayed if she'd wanted to, she had moved away. She had gone to live in an entirely different kind of place. She had, come to think of it, taken up with an entirely different kind of man.

A big change, Sader thought—you might say, almost overnight.

It was almost as if Tina Champlain had become a different woman.

CHAPTER SIX

In Westwood Village, Sader went into a drugstore phone booth and called Mr. Twining. Mr. Twining expressed his regret at having sent Sader on a wild goose chase, and he said that there was another woman who had been a member of the Women's Circle for years, and who should certainly be at home, as she was temporarily invalided following an automobile accident.

The house was in the hills north of the university. He explained to Sader how to find the street.

The house was sheltered by a trio of big eucalyptus. It was much like the Forrest place, about as big, and Sader had begun to get an idea of the sort of flock Mr. Twining guided. You wouldn't get anywhere here, Sader thought, being a Holy Roller. These people would go for a dignified, liberal faith, a quiet service, and if anybody got the spirit and was seized with a desire to holler over it, he would be efficiently taken out. He rang Mrs. Bowen's doorbell and a pleasant-looking chocolate-colored maid let him in. It seemed that Mr. Twining had already telephoned.

She was a very thin woman in a wheel chair, wearing a pink silk robe and with a white knitted coverlet about her legs. Gray hair, glasses, and an expression that made Sader suspect her husband gambled or drank, and that she forgave him for it. She let Sader sit down on a needle-point chair. "Mr. Twining tells me you're trying to find the Champlains' child."

"Yes, that's right."

"You are a private detective?" Gambling or drunk, Mr. Bowen would have a hard time keeping anything from her sharp eyes.

"Yes, ma'am."

"I won't question you, prying into your affairs. I know that you detectives have to keep secrets, you can't discuss your client's business. I watch Perry Mason on TV every week," she added.

"Well, we want to locate the baby because of an inheritance." He had said it so often that now it sounded like the truth.

"That may be. What do you want me to tell you? I might explain that I wasn't well acquainted with Mr. Champlain, merely to speak to at church. I knew Mrs. Champlain through our Women's Circle. Really, what I know about them is mostly secondhand, what I happened to hear from other people."

Cagey, Sader thought, in case I try to pin her down. Perry's footwork must be contagious. "Would you have any idea who might be keeping Mrs. Champlain's child?"

"I'm afraid not." She sat quiet then, as if thinking this over. Across the room on a marble mantelpiece was a silver clock with a loud, peaceful tick. The hands stood at twelve minutes past ten. "There was an aunt. I met her at one of our missionary luncheons. The name was—wait a minute—" Sader waited; he felt like holding his breath. "—Shawell. I'm sure of it. I remember, I asked her how to spell it. From the way Mrs. Champlain had pronounced it, I thought the word had been *shawl*. You know." She touched the knitted wrapping on her knees. "It seemed an odd name, and she spelled it for me."

"Shawell."

"Perhaps the aunt has the baby."

"Could you describe her?"

"She seemed like a very nice person," Mrs. Bowen said, with so much emphasis that Sader wanted to pop back with *Who said she wasn't?*

"I mean," he explained, "was she tall? Thin? Well dressed? Or what?"

"She was . . . oh, just medium height. I don't recall much about her features, nor about her appearance in general, except that—" She hitched the knitted cover closer, laced a finger in its fringe. "What I have to say, Mr. Sader —we're not gossips. We don't meet every week to tear other women to tatters, though that's the old cliché, the thing they always do in jokes and cartoons. We make clothes and quilts for the missions and we talk—we try to talk as Christians should. What was said about Mrs. Shawell, and I agreed with it, was that she seemed like such a *country* sort of woman."

Sader just sat there looking at her.

"I see you don't quite know what I mean. Perhaps I

shouldn't even have mentioned it. She was a little bit dowdy. And she spoke with an accent. Not much of an accent, just a little."

Just enough to be different, Sader thought. "I believe Mrs. Champlain's people live in eastern Canada, that both she and Mr. Champlain were of French descent. Perhaps that would account for the aunt's accent."

"Probably it would."

"Did you know that Mrs. Champlain was dead?" Sader asked, taking off for no reason on a new tack.

"Not until Mr. Twining told me, just before you came."

"She hadn't kept in touch with anyone at the church?"

"No. Not at all. That happens sometimes. When something terrible happens, when a loved one is lost, sometimes faith goes too."

"Yes, I guess that's true."

"I was so terribly surprised that it was Mrs. Champlain who was dead," Mrs. Bowen went on. "When Mr. Twining first began to speak, when I caught the name Champlain and understood that there had been a death, I was sure he must be speaking of the Champlain baby. During the last months she went to St. John's, she spoke often of the baby's illness."

Sader must have looked his surprise. "I hadn't heard of this."

"She was . . . it had something to do with a heart defect."

"She must have been taking the baby to a doctor," Sader said, thinking of the avenue thus opened.

"She may have. I don't know."

"Is there anyone else I could see, anyone of your Women's Circle, who was a close friend? Who might know where the child is now?"

"I don't believe so, Mr. Sader. Mrs. Champlain cut herself off from all of us at St. John's. Perhaps it was somewhat our fault, too. We were all busy with our own affairs, and we—we just sort of let her go." Her tone seemed full of a genuine regret.

From some rear part of the house, Sader heard the squeals and cries of children, suddenly raised. Mrs. Bowen flinched, her mouth puckering; then she shrugged as if in resignation. "It's hard for me to be patient over the noise, since—" She forced a smile, ruefully. "I'm not a very good invalid, I'm afraid."

Judging by her appearance, Sader thought, Mrs. Bowen must have married and borne her children later than most. "At least you can keep them out from underfoot with a house this size."

"Yes. And Ada—she let you in—she's very helpful with them."

"How many children have you?" Sader was rising to leave.

She hesitated for a moment. "It sounds like a dozen, doesn't it? But there are only three."

Among the children, one had started to cry. "Seems as if there might have been a fight," Sader offered.

"Mr. Sader, that goes on all day long."

The chocolate-colored maid ushered him to the front door and said a polite good-bye. Her brown eyes were still watching him as he got behind the wheel of the car, and

Sader decided she thought that private detectives weren't to be trusted and wanted to make sure that he was leaving the premises.

There were no Shawells listed in any of the five Metropolitan L.A. phone books. Sader drove downtown to the Main Library then and searched the city directories. There were a couple of Shawells, one in Hollywood, and he drove there, thinking it the logical choice because it wasn't too far from West L.A. The place was in a narrow block below Hollywood Boulevard, where old cottages had been taken over by photographers, arch-support dealers and truss manufacturers, a vanity publisher and a shoe-repair shop. The address he wanted was at the rear, an apartment over garages, and when he had climbed the stairs he found a name typed on a card, RHODA K. SHAWELL, and below the name written in red ink, *Metaphysics*.

Again Sader had the ominous, lurching sense of a loss of footing, and the rage-making frustration. Everywhere he turned in this thing, he ended in a blind alley. In that moment Tina Champlain and her child had no more reality for him than a puff of smoke. He was chasing and running after a couple of ghosts.

He put a finger on the bell and kept it there, because he was mad, and when the door was flung open he stared in at her with such a look that she stepped back, almost flinching.

She wasn't the aunt. She had brilliantly dyed red-gold hair and a tangle of bead bracelets, a blue silk blouse tight across the bust and blue capri pants. She could have been forty, or sixty, under the pancake makeup and the rouge, but the accent was pure Brooklyn when she asked, "What can I do for you, mister?"

"You're Mrs. Shawell?"

"Says so on the door, doesn't it?"

"Are you related to a woman named Tina Champlain?"

She blinked, the lashes heavy with mascara. The bead bracelets tinkled as she lifted a hand to fluff the brilliant hair. "I never heard the name before in my life, mister. Is there anything else?"

"Not a thing, thanks."

He ran down the steps and she hollered after him, "You meet all kinds out here in Hollywood, I always say."

"Amen," Sader flung over his shoulder.

At the curb, reaching for a cigarette before getting into the car, Sader saw that his hands were shaking. *Papa*, he said to himself, echoing Scarborough's name for him when he betrayed himself, *Papa, you're getting your personal feelings mixed up in this thing and that isn't going to be good for anybody. Not even for Tina's kid.* He lighted the cigarette and got into the car and pulled out of the slot and north toward Hollywood Boulevard. He took the freeway into town, cut into the Santa Ana freeway eastward. The second Shawell lived out in Whittier, the village founded by the Friends and now grown into a brash upstart of a young city. The street, when Sader found it, might have been preserved intact out of the past. The homes were old and quiet, magnolias and elms were tall. The overcast had broken a little, there were patches of weak sunshine.

Sader stood on the sidewalk and looked at the house,

having no hope at all that the Shawell here would be Tina Champlain's relative. He went up the walk which was bordered with begonias, and rang the bell. The door opened in a minute or so, and he saw a teen-ager in jeans and pony tail.

"Is Mrs. Shawell here?"

"Mrs. . . ? Oh, you mean Aunt Louise. Come in. I'll get her."

The front door opened into an entry with a hall beyond. The young girl led the way, pony tail swinging, on into the living room. It was large and old-fashioned, rather dark because the windows were heavily draped, and with three big bouquets of roses on a couple of tables and the mantel. The roses must have been fresh-picked that morning since the odor was dewy rather than sweet.

When the older woman entered, Sader turned to look at her. She was at least fifty, she wore blue gingham with a white cotton apron and there were flour marks above her wrists. She had a strong, square face. Dark eyes and brows. When he saw her he had the first hunch of having hit what he was looking for, since Gibbings had entered his office. "Mrs. Shawell? Are you related to Tina Champlain?"

"I'm her aunt."

A prickle of nervous hope ran through Sader like an electric current. "Could we talk for a minute?"

"Of course. Have a chair. That one."

There was an accent all right, the sort you might have if you'd grown up thinking in one language and having occasionally to speak in another. It was, Sader thought, more of a hesitation than an accent, the sense of choice among half-familiar words. "I'm a private investigator. My name's Sader. I'd like to ask a few questions about Mrs. Champlain, about what has become of her little boy."

She was sitting opposite, a dozen feet away, her hands folded on her lap. Sader wished that the room were brighter. She seemed to be at a loss, and he couldn't see her eyes under the fringe of lash.

"Do you know where Mrs. Champlain's child is now? Who's keeping him?"

A half-dozen words from her, Sader told himself, and he'd know and the job would be done. Less than a minute, less than half a minute. She lifted the dark eyes and Sader leaned forward and then she said, "Who sent you here to ask?"

There was no use giving her the line about money coming through the mother, Sader thought. He said, "I'm sorry, I can't tell you. I would appreciate it if you'd tell me where he is."

"Mr. Sader, he wasn't really Tina's child. She had no right to him."

"We know that the child wasn't actually hers," Sader answered. "But we want to find him anyway. Do you know where he is?"

She was shaking her head, and Sader felt like cursing. "He was not the . . . one does not hate a child for it, but—" She added a French phrase in a half-whisper.

She was thinking of the illegitimacy. "Your niece couldn't have children of her own," Sader pointed out reasonably, "and she was perfectly within her rights to adopt a baby. Her husband approved."

She made an explosive sound of protest, but Sader went on.

"She loved the baby, provided for it, cared for it. If you know where the child is now, if you loved your niece and want to do what she would want you to, you'll tell me where the little boy is."

"I don't know."

"When did you see him last?"

He could sense her unwillingness. She looked at the hall, as if something in the kitchen perhaps required her attention. "A week, ten days maybe, after Tina was drowned, I went to Tina's house, and there was an old lady with the baby, and nothing to eat and no money to pay her with."

Sader couldn't believe his ears. "You hadn't gone until then? Knowing that your niece was dead, the baby was alone?"

"I didn't know about . . . about her dying, right away. Not as soon as it happened." She sat stiffened on the chair; the dark eyes defied him. "I went as soon as I could. There was nothing I could do, nothing more."

"What about the other relatives? The other aunt, the uncle?"

She looked briefly puzzled, perhaps at his knowing about them. "My sister and her husband went back to Canada a long time ago."

"I don't understand this situation," Sader said, trying to control his rising temper. "There was money left to Mrs. Champlain, a lot of insurance money, after her husband died on that plane."

"There was some money," Mrs. Shawell admitted grudgingly, "but then there was the funeral, and she loaned some of it to her friend, the friend who builds boats."

News he hadn't heard from the Perrines, Sader noted. "But that still wouldn't account for all of it. The baby should have been rich in his own right, rich enough anyway to hire an old lady and to buy something to eat. Who took charge of him?"

The black eyes glittered, almost with a look of tears, and he thought for a moment she wasn't going to answer. Then she said almost whispering: "He wasn't Tina's child, he didn't belong to her."

"Do you mean," Sader said, "that you abandoned him? That none of you offered him a home? You left him there in that condemned house with an old woman who hadn't even been paid for keeping him? With nothing to eat?"

She was silent, and Sader added, "I just can't believe it."

She must have seen the contemptuous look he gave the room, measuring its spacious comfort, for she said, "I wasn't living here then. I had a rented room. This is my nephew's home."

Sader bent his gaze on her again. "Mrs. Champlain's father is alive, I understand. Didn't he feel called upon to protect her little boy?"

"Not . . . not . . ." She was agitated, trembling. She threw out her hands as if the situation was past explaining. "No."

"You don't know who has the little boy? No idea at all?"

She spoke all in a rush. "The old lady said that the father

had come to see him. The father was going to take him away."

Again Sader felt like shaking his head to get the sand out of his ears. "Mrs. Champlain's father?"

"*The baby's father.*"

He felt like an idiot or a parrot, repeating it over again. "The baby's father had come to get him?"

"Yes."

Sader drew a deep breath. There was still a chance here, she could still say a half-dozen words and end it for him. "And who is he? What is his name?"

She let him hope for a moment, then she answered. "I don't know his name. I don't know anything about him. Just that he came . . . and said he would come back."

The air of the room seemed blotted with stuffiness, and the smell of the roses made Sader sick.

CHAPTER SEVEN

Frimm, Watley and Stone, Architects, had their own building on the Wilshire Boulevard corner, a three-story monolith of orange glass, blue tile and pebbled aluminum, with opalescent window lights in a hop-skip design, all tautly modernistic. Either it had been occupied before it had been completely built, or Frimm, Watley and Stone couldn't resist architectural afterthoughts. There was scaffolding around the lower floor and a clutter of glass and steel on the sidewalk, waiting to be used.

Sader went in through the boarded entry. A small tiled lobby was cleared, and there was a shiny stairway beyond. Past the stairway, the interior looked like an excavated cave. No work seemed to be in progress at the moment. Some planks had been laid across a couple of sawhorses to form a table, and here were blueprints spread out and a pair of men looking them over. Neither of the men were Gibbings, so Sader went on upstairs.

There was nothing unfinished here. The carpeting was deep and the receptionist's desk was mahogany. The receptionist had lavender lips, silver fingernails, a size thirty-nine bust, nice dimples, and she was pretty. Her blonde hair needed touching up at the roots but on her it looked intriguing. "Mr. Gibbings? Do you have an appointment to see him?"

"Please just tell him Sader is here."

She tapped the big desk with the silver nails and let him see the dimples. "Do you mind telling me your business with Mr. Gibbings?"

"I don't mind a bit," Sader said, "but he'd break our necks."

The dimples went away. "Just a moment, please." She pushed buttons on a matching mahogany box and spoke into it secretively. Then she rose. "This way, please." She led him down the carpeted hall and opened a door. Gibbings looked up; he was behind a desk with some big sheets of paper spread out before him. As Sader got closer he saw that they were architectural drawings.

"Well, sit down. I didn't tell you to come here, by the way."

"I know you didn't." Sader sat down in a leather chair. "I have to know how far you want me to go. That's why I came."

There was, if possible, even less humor visible in Gibbings than Sader had found yesterday. The old eyes were glacial, and Gibbings seemed to have drawn to himself an air of authority from his rich surroundings. "You've heard of telephones?"

"I've heard of switchboard girls listening in, too. To get to the point: from what information I've gained so far, the baby seems to have been taken by the father. Do you still want me to find him?"

Sader couldn't see any change at all in the old man's manner. The mention of the man who must have wrecked his daughter's life didn't even raise a flush. "I've hired you to find him. I've paid a decent retainer. Are you detectives always so squeamish about getting to the end of the job?"

"You don't intend to claim the kid?"

"I said so."

"What *are* you going to do?"

"I'll decide that when you can tell me where he is." Gibbings made a few doodling marks with a pencil on the edge of one of the drawings. "Did you see Wanda Nevins?"

"She seems to think that I don't know exactly what I'm doing."

Gibbings' smile was sudden, harsh, and wintry. "And *do* you know, Mr. Sader?"

"I have the feeling you haven't been honest with me. No, it's not really that," Sader corrected, "it's more of a feeling that there is something you haven't told me. A big chunk of the truth. Is there any chance I might get to talk to your daughter?"

"Not a chance on earth."

"Well, then, it's up to you to supply the name of the man who fathered her child. I have to have that much from you."

Gibbings swung his big chair around so that he half-faced a window. The light from the opalescent glass illuminated the planes of his face, etching dark lines in every wrinkle, and Sader thought that he looked at least a hundred. "What did I tell you in our interview yesterday?"

"You said that your daughter was in love with a young soldier who had died in Japan before they could marry. Mr. Gibbings, I know that yarn can't be the truth."

Gibbings had actually flinched, as if Sader's bald account had jarred him. He made a few more doodles with an absent air, not looking over at Sader, and then he said, "Would you believe me if I told you that—no matter what anyone else has said—this man doesn't have the child?"

"I'd expect you to explain why he doesn't."

Gibbings thought about it. The office was very quiet. Sader wondered why they had torn up the lower floor, and what they were going to do with it. And why Mr. Gibbings didn't want a grandson—even an illegitimate grandson—to carry on in the firm. The kid could be brought in under another name, educated, given the chance he deserved.

"He doesn't have the baby because he never knew it existed," said Gibbings heavily.

"He died without knowing?"

Gibbings' mouth had the shape of a shark's. "He lives without knowing."

"And your daughter? Does she know what became of her baby?"

For some unfathomable reason it hit home. Sader was startled. The old man blanched white, and the pouches under his eye sockets had the hue of scorched flesh. He swallowed a couple of times, Sader watching his throat work, and then he stammered, "I'll explain just this much. My daughter is an invalid. A shut-in—that's supposed to make it sound nicer. You see, the baby was fine after it was born, but Kit wasn't. She was past the age for easy childbirth, and then something about the spinal anesthesia went wrong. She lost the use of her legs. Not right away, but gradually. You'll never meet her, Mr. Sader. You will never ask her a single question. You will just please find this child about whom the letter was written, and bring the address to me. And that's all."

Sader got up and went to the door. He looked at Gibbings back of the big desk. "I feel awfully sorry for your daughter. I think she got a real rotten deal all the way around." He opened the door and went out and shut it behind him. Gibbings said something in a half-shout just as the door closed but Sader didn't pause. He passed the receptionist; she had a small mirror and a lavender lipstick in her hands. She glanced at Sader, started to drop them into a drawer, then decided he wasn't important enough to matter. She began a hasty lip repair job.

Ralph Perrine peered at Sader through the screen. The screen was fuzzy with dust; perhaps he didn't see Sader too well. The afternoon sun had come out a little stronger, and from the rain-dampened yard behind the house came the smells of wet wood and varnish. Nearer at hand, on the other side of the screen, was the odor of muscatel. Perrine rubbed the disordered gray hair from his eyes and grunted, "Oh . . . uh . . . it's you again."

"It's me," Sader agreed. "I've got to see your son."

"He isn't here." Perrine sniffled and drew a hand across his nose. He'd been hitting it, he wasn't the same man Sader had encountered yesterday. "What do you want with him, anyhow?"

"I have to have the name of the woman who took care of Mrs. Champlain's baby when he and she went out on dates." Sader got close enough to the screen to see the wavering eyes. "In case you know it—"

"I don't. No. Maybe Brent don't even know it, now. Maybe he forgot it."

"I'd like to ask him."

"He's out buying something or other for one of the boats."

"I'll wait, then."

There was a moment of hesitation. Then Perrine started to open the screen. He pushed it out an inch or so and then changed his mind. "Well, might as well go look. He could of come back by now." Perrine came out on the porch. He still wore what he'd had on yesterday, the tired shirt and the work pants, but they showed in indefinable ways that he had slept in them. He looked rumpled and dilapidated, and Sader judged that he'd drunk his way through the night and what was gone of the day. He sniffled on his hand again, and stumbled down the front steps, around the house to the back yard.

Sader noticed a can of white paint, the lid off, spilled in the dusty grass. Perrine seemed to notice it at the same time. He grunted in anger, or surprise, and went to it and tipped it upright with his shoe. Then Sader noticed something else, a long splintered mark along the freshly painted prow of the near hull.

He went closer, put a finger into the narrow groove. The mark had been made on a surface not yet dried. The broken splinters were still damp to the touch.

The white paintbrush lay about ten feet beyond, at the edge of some piled tarps and other gear. To Sader the silence suddenly took on an empty quality, a sort of waiting. He looked back at old man Perrine, who was rubbing his nose and staring at the marked hull.

Sader walked past the stern of the hull, to the heap of gear. Behind it Brent Perrine sat on the ground, doubled over, gripping his thigh. Sader jumped a couple of coiled hawsers and bent over him. Brent looked up, a grimace twisting his lips so that his big white teeth showed. "Get me something. A towel, anything. My damned leg's bleeding."

The pants leg was soaked red and there were thick drops spattered below Brent's lifted knee.

The father stumbled past Sader and his son kicked out at him with his good leg. "Goddam you, didn't you hear me yelling?"

"Didn't hear nothing."

Sader turned back to the house, went up the stairs to the kitchen, looked in some cupboard drawers. He found a clean dishcloth, went back out to the yard. But Brent waved him off. "I'd better go inside. I don't want the neighbors staring."

Sader glanced around. There were no houses near. To the south was an empty lot with a FOR SALE sign in it, littered with weeds and cans. To the north was the brick wall of a machine shop. Long ago someone had built the old house, probably in the middle of a block of lawn, with the hopes that other big homes would be built to neighbor it; but all that had happened was that it had sat alone for a long time and then the block had been split into lots and sold.

The old man leaned down toward Brent, and Brent grabbed him savagely and forced himself to his feet. He tried to walk, but then Sader had to help. The three of them staggered in zigzags toward the back porch while Brent cursed under his breath. At the steps Sader took a quick look backward and saw the red splashes here and there, bright in the dead grass, but not too many; and he judged that the bleeding must be subsiding. He had left the dishcloth out there; he made a mental note of this excuse to go back later.

In the kitchen Brent flopped on a chair and clutched his leg, making a hissing noise between his teeth. His father got a pair of scissors out of a drawer and came wandering over to pluck at the blood-soaked pants leg, and Brent yelled at him, "Goddam it, do you want to ruin the pants too? Wait'll I get them off."

Old man Perrine said blearily, "There's a couple of holes in them already."

Brent was wriggling, pulling the pants loose from his waist.

Sader said, "Somebody took a shot at you. Either they're a rotten shot, or they only meant to scare you. The bullet ricocheted off the hull and hit you down there." Brent had the pants down around his shoes and was staring at the inside of his left thigh. There was a long, bleeding gouge in the flesh that made Sader think of the mark on the hull. "Well, it didn't do much more than nick you."

"It bled like hell," Brent said, relief in his tone. He had thought it would be a lot worse, obviously. "Hey, I won't need a doctor or anything. Just antiseptic and bandages."

"Get a tetanus shot just to be safe," Sader told him.

Brent's eyes were losing their ferocious, shocked look. "Yeah, yeah. Dad, bring me the first-aid kit. It's in the hall closet, the top shelf."

Sader said, "Aren't you kind of curious about who shot you?"

The room got quiet suddenly. Old man Perrine had started for the hall, and he stopped, and looked at Sader as if Sader had just made some unpardonably rude remark. The anger came back into Brent's face.

"People who aren't afraid to try to scare you that way might not be afraid to aim better next time," Sader pointed out.

"I want any advice from you, I'll ask you for it."

Sader shrugged, turned to the kitchen door.

"Where are you going?" Brent demanded.

"I left something out there."

"You damned well leave it, then." He must have felt a twinge of pain from his wound at this point, for he flinched and put an involuntary hand down. "What did you come for, anyway?"

"I need the name of the woman who stayed with Mrs. Champlain's baby when she went out with you."

"I don't remember it."

Sader moved away from the door, found a chair and sat down.

Brent said, "Mrs. Cecil. She lived next door."

"First name?"

"I don't know. I really don't know. Tina always called her Mrs. Cecil. She was a gray-haired old lady, had a son living nearby. Maybe she's moved in with him."

"Did Tina Champlain ever say anything to you about the baby's father? Not her husband. I mean the real father. That he'd ever come around, or she'd seen him? Anything at all?"

"Hell, no. I don't think she knew anything about the baby's real parents."

Sader wondered if Tina Champlain had deliberately given this impression or if it was something Brent had mistakenly taken for granted.

Ralph Perrine came back carrying a white tin box, put it on the floor by Brent's chair, opened it to expose packed medications and rolls of gauze and adhesive tape. He fumbled for a small bottle of iodine, began to unscrew the cap. Sader rose as if to leave.

Brent motioned to him. "Wait a minute. How're you coming with this job of yours?"

"I'm still looking."

"It shouldn't be too hard to find the kid. Did you locate Tina's aunt?"

"I talked to her but she doesn't know who has the baby. She seems to think Mrs. Champlain made a big mistake in taking him. I got the impression the whole family washed its hands of him as soon as Tina Champlain died." Sader was watching Brent for any reaction, but Brent was now engrossed in caring for his wound. He had yanked the bottle of antiseptic away from the old man and had begun to run the applicator against the gouged mark in his thigh. It must have hurt badly, for he stopped almost at once and sat there, the painful grimace on his face again.

Sader tried again. "This elderly woman who was caring for the baby told the aunt—according to the aunt's story—that the baby's real father was coming to get him. I can't help wondering: How would she know the real father if she saw him? Providing even Mrs. Champlain didn't know him?"

"It sounds screwy," Brent said; but Sader caught the note of caution in his voice and guessed that Brent was thinking it through and adding it to other things already known.

"If the baby's father had contacted Mrs. Champlain, would she have mentioned it to you?"

"Hell, yes," Brent said at once. His father had opened another bottle of medicine, had dipped a cotton swab into it. As he inched over to touch the red wound with the swab, Brent balled a fist and hit him right below the collarbone, and sent him spinning. "You goddam old wino, leave me be."

The air seemed to crackle with hatred and fury.

Sader kept calm. "When you were going with Mrs. Champlain, engaged to her, did you ever talk about adopting the baby after the marriage?"

"Yeah, we talked about it."

"Did you check on the little boy after she died?"

"I figured that was her folks' business." Brent was leaning over the wounded leg, staring at the old man. Ralph

Perrine was crouched in injured silence, the open bottle dribbling antiseptic through his fingers.

"Did you like the kid?"

"Look, goddam it, leave me alone. I've told you all I know. Sure, I liked the kid okay. What's to like about a five-year-old kid? He's just there, that's all. This one wasn't sassy and he kept out of my way and if Tina wanted him it was okay by me."

"Who hated her enough to take the child and abuse him after she died?"

It seemed to jerk Brent up short. He quit glaring at his father and turned a blank, angry stare on Sader. "Who? Nobody. You must be nuts, thinking a thing like that."

Sader shook his head. He opened the door and went out. Out at the boat, he studied the mark on the freshly painted hull. He didn't find any spent bullet, though it must have been there somewhere.

From inside the house there was a noise as if a chair had crashed, or had hit a wall, and Sader waited; but there was nothing more. The Perrines were settling their disagreement privately.

He tried to figure, from the angle of the mark on the hull, where the person holding the gun had stood, but this was fruitless. The bullet had been sharply deflected on striking the hardwood surface, it had gouged an irregular channel and been further deflected by the cross grain. He couldn't even make out where Perrine had been, though he had a hunch that Perrine had somehow been warned, had thrown the paint bucket and brush off into the grass as he had run. There was the whole stretch of trampled grass, the back of the house, the vacant lot next door—the shot could have come from any of these.

The poor aim might have simply been an accident, the effort of trying to hit a running target, and Brent Perrine might be in much more danger than he himself seemed to suppose.

CHAPTER EIGHT

By the time Sader got to Santa Monica the sun was in the west, dipping into a fog bank out across the Pacific. He could smell and feel the sea, without being able to see it. The mountainous heap of earth that was to be a freeway seemed poised over the wrecked houses like the blunt end of an avalanche. There was no sign of its having been worked on during the day. Sader concluded that they were waiting for the land to be cleared. He got out of his car and walked around Tina Champlain's house, went out into the back yard and even peered into the trash barrel. The ashy smell of the old incinerator tainted the air. He had no purpose but the faint desire to delay coming to grips with a handful of feathers.

The only Cecil living in this part of Santa Monica was a Lloyd Cecil, two blocks over. He drove there, parked, got out again. It was a block of small neat homes, not new but pretty well kept. The sort of neighborhood where people exchanged plant cuttings, so that everyone had a patch of ivy geraniums out by the curb, and almost everybody had elephant's ear and jacobinia by the porch, like a thread woven from yard to yard. Sader went to the door and knocked. An elderly woman opened it, almost at once.

"Mrs. Cecil?"

"That's right."

"Are you the Mrs. Cecil who used to take care of Mrs. Champlain's baby?"

"Yes, I am."

"Would you happen to know who has him? Where he is now?"

"I believe I do."

She spoke calmly, confidently, and looked at him directly through her steel-rimmed specs, but Sader wanted to chew his lips and scratch himself. Frustration had become a habit and he was wary of letting it go. People in this affair didn't just come out and offer to tell you things, and he almost disliked her for offering to do it.

"Where is he?"

"I'll have to look up the address. Would you like to come in and wait while I find it?"

He went in. The room was small, and furnished in an ordinary way. In the dining room, past an archway, he saw an oversized painting hung on the wall, a stag at bay with a bunch of wolves, full of blood and snow; and he thought it was a rather odd decoration and then remembered that his grandmother had kept a large oil of a trio of dead ducks and hunting paraphernalia on her own wall and right where Sader had had to look at it when he had been taken to her house for dinner. The ducks had seemed terribly defunct to Sader's young eyes.

Mrs. Cecil had padded to a built-in cabinet beside the gas log fireplace and opened a glass-paned door and taken out a cardboard box. She adjusted the specs on her nose and lifted the box lid, took out some papers, set the box in the cupboard, and began to read. After scrutinizing a half-dozen odd-sized scraps she said, "Now I just know it's here someplace," and Sader felt the familiar disappointment and thought of Tina's little boy, waiting somewhere to be found.

Maybe hungry at this minute, or afraid.

But then she had it. "Down the coast, near Laguna." She twitched the paper toward the light and read aloud Wanda Nevins' address.

Sader wanted to yank the scrap of paper from her hands, verify what he had heard, but instead he said, "May I sit down?"

She looked at him over the specs. "Why, sure, go ahead." Her manner implied that she was surprised he wasn't ready to go, since she'd given him what he wanted. Sader made note of the lack of curiosity, or any question about himself. "Do you mind telling me about the person who came to get the baby?"

"He was the baby's father." She was growing a little uncertain, but still held the scrap of paper as if it might have what Sader wanted.

"I mean, a description. How he looked, the name he gave. A car, if he drove one."

Her eyes lit up behind the specs. "He drove a very nice car."

"Do you remember the make and the year?"

"Oh, no. I don't drive and I know very little about cars. But it was red and it was the kind you can put the top down."

A red convertible, Sader made note, adding a private bet that it had been rented. "And what was he like?"

"Mr. Nevins? Well, he was tall and—"

"Wait a minute." Sader had almost jumped out of the chair. "*Mr. Nevins?*"

She nodded, looking a little anxious now. "Why, yes. Is anything wrong? He seemed like such a nice man to me."

"Did you ever meet a friend of Mrs. Champlain's named Wanda Nevins?"

She blinked, even more disturbed now. "No. Is she a relative of Mr. Nevins?"

"I don't know." Sader felt absolutely flabbergasted and knew that it showed in his face.

"I didn't meet many of Mrs. Champlain's friends," Mrs. Cecil explained. "Mostly I stayed with the little boy when she went out with her gentleman friend. That was Mr. Perrine. He has a boat-building place in Wilmington. That is, I believe he has a regular job and the boat-building is something he does on the side. Mrs. Champlain mentioned it to me. If they'd got married, he was going into the boat-building full time."

"This man who came to the house and said he was the baby's real father . . . he couldn't have been Brent Perrine?"

"Oh, no," she cried, as if Sader must be crazy. "I *know* Mr. Perrine. I met his father, too. It wasn't either of them. I told you, it was Mr. Nevins!"

"When was the first time the baby's father came?"

She was growing uneasy. She retreated cautiously to a chair and sat down, fingering the bit of paper. "When he first got here, I remember I was crying. I was still upset over hearing about Mrs. Champlain. She was drowned on a Saturday. He must have come on the next day, Sunday, late on Sunday. They phoned me from Catalina on Sunday morning, Mr. Perrine's father telling me they couldn't find her. I cried all day. Every time I looked at Ricky and thought about his mother being dead, I started crying all over again."

Sader flinched, thinking: *Ricky*. It was the first time he had heard the boy's name. Up to now Tina Champlain's child had had a certain anonymity, a lack of substance now supplied by the name, and having him thus identified made Sader want to squirm. A kid named Ricky had hunger and pain that was real. You couldn't endure thinking of the child's body subjected to abuse; the tears were warm and wet, and the sobs were something you heard if you stopped to listen. "When this man came, did he know that Mrs. Champlain was dead?"

The question seemed to startle her. "Why, I . . . I suppose so. I must have blurted something out as soon as he came to the door. I must have explained why I was crying like that."

"So you don't really know whether he had heard of her death, or not?"

"No. . . ." She hesitated. "Wouldn't he have acted surprised, though?"

"Perhaps. How did he seem with the little boy? Fatherly?"

She straightened the edge of a rag rug with her toe. "That part of it was kind of awkward. Ricky didn't know him and he acted scared, he ran and tried to hide under the bed."

"What did you do?"

"I had Mr. Nevins sit down and I brought out some lemonade and chocolate cake. Pretty soon Ricky came back, and I gave him a glass of lemonade and got him to eat some cake, and then he didn't seem so frightened."

"Do you think Ricky had any idea he was adopted? Of course he was young to try to explain—"

"Of course not! Why, I didn't know myself, not to be certain. I used to wonder a little, some of the things I saw in the house, the baby things—"

"What did this man Nevins say to you? Why had he come at this time? What were his plans for the little boy?" Sader wanted to rush her along, pry all the truth from her in one lump. "Did he seem like the kind of man you'd *want* to turn the child over to?"

"Yes—I—" She seemed to bristle, the eyes behind the steel-rimmed lenses glowed with resentment. "Who are you? What's the idea of making out like I was in the wrong? Are you a relative, you want the little boy for yourself?"

Sader thought that it was late for this kind of curiosity from her. Either she'd been busy covering something, some secret or a lie, or she was simply a very gullible old lady. "My name is Sader and I'm a detective."

"I haven't done anything wrong. I don't have to be afraid of the law."

"I'm not the law. I'm a private detective. I've taken on the job of finding the little boy."

Her pudgy hands were clenched. "I've told you where to find him."

"I went to that house," Sader said grimly, "and there aren't any kids in it."

"Well . . . I did what I thought best," she stammered. There was something almost infantile in her fright. She was like an ancient child accused of a fault she couldn't comprehend. "He was the boy's father and he wanted Ricky back."

"Let me tell *you* how it was," Sader said. "You were at the house alone with the boy, the mother was dead. No husband, either. You had no idea who might show up to take the kid off your hands, nor how long you'd be required to stay with him, unpaid perhaps. This man who said he was Ricky's father came and you believed him, perhaps with some reservations. If he had wanted to take the little boy away at that time, you might have asked for identification, some proof that he was who he said he was. But he didn't take the kid, and then he didn't come back right away. Mrs. Champlain's aunt went to the house a week or ten days after her death and you were still there, with nothing to eat and no one offering to pay you for your time."

Mrs. Cecil had begun to nod in a stricken sort of way.

"When this man, this so-called father, came back he must have looked like a godsend. You knew from the aunt that Mrs. Champlain's family had discarded the little boy like a piece of trash. You must have been pretty desperate."

Some of the fright left her face, and she drew a long relaxing breath.

"I'm not blaming you at all, Mrs. Cecil. No one could. You were in a tough spot. You were doing more for the kid than the mother's family—hell, they'd abandoned him. Even so, you must have begun to think of calling on Juvenile Hall."

She shook her head. "I hated to do that."

Sader made note of the phrase, remembering Brent Perrine's description of the quiet self-effacing little boy. Mrs. Cecil had been very fond of Ricky. He would have bet that when Tina's cupboard had finally been bare, food was brought from her own house. "Of course you kept hoping that this man would come back, and then he did, and your troubles were over. I have reason to think that Ricky's were just beginning."

"What do you mean?"

"My client thinks Ricky is being abused, wherever he is. I want you to tell me everything about this father of his that you can remember. Every scrap."

Now the fright had changed to apprehension. "Ricky isn't treated right?"

"Just tell me about this Mr. Nevins."

"He said he was Ricky's father."

"And Ricky tried to crawl under the bed."

"Well, he was shy. A quiet, shy little boy. He never made up with strangers. When I kept him I never had to worry that he'd get out and let someone take him into their car. Like, you know, a fiend or something."

"I see."

She frowned, trying to concentrate. "He didn't look

much like Ricky. I remember how that struck me. Ricky is slender and small, dark hair, and this man was tall and very blond. He had the kind of hair—well, you see it at the beach. Sun-streaked. And he was tanned."

"The outdoor type," Sader said. "How was he dressed?"

"Very nicely. My son's always liked good clothes, and I've learned to judge men's things a little. My husband . . . well, he was a working man. Jimmy's in an office, he has to look neat. I thought at the time, when Ricky's father first came, that he must be making good money because his clothes were so good and then he had the car. It looked expensive."

"When did he finally take Ricky away?"

"Two weeks to the day that Mrs. Champlain had drowned."

"Did he ever offer any explanation as to why he first showed up when he did?"

She was obviously trying hard, sorting the fading memories. "He said that Ricky had been given away without his permission."

"Did he mention Ricky's mother, the real mother?"

"No. I noticed that."

Was it possible that Gibbings was wrong, that the man Kit Gibbings had loved did know about the child, and that this Nevins was he? Then Sader thought of the proper question. "How old was he?"

"He was awfully young, I mean to be Ricky's father. I said something to him, some remark about how old he'd been when Ricky was born, and he said he had been seventeen."

That knocks it, Sader thought. This wasn't Kit Gibbings' sweetheart. This man had been a fake. Someone sent to claim Tina Champlain's little boy. But *why*? For God's sake, why? To take the kid away to starve him, to beat and degrade him? Sader had the buffeting sensation of having caught the tail end of a nightmare.

"The second time he came he brought Ricky a present. I guess that's why I decided to trust him," Mrs. Cecil said on a note of apology, as if Sader was going to tell her she'd done wrong.

Sader lifted an eyebrow and she added, "A Chinese puzzle sort of thing, a funny little pugnose dog made out of bits of wood. You took him apart and then you tried to put him together again."

"A Chinese puzzle." Sader was thinking of the big Buddha in Wanda's living room, the Oriental arrangement and furnishings.

"It was too old for Ricky, he couldn't figure it out."

It could mean a link, or nothing. It could mean that someone was unfamiliar with the tastes of five-year-olds.

"Did this man make any promises about letting you see Ricky again? Bringing him back for a visit? A phone call?"

"No . . . except as he left, he said, 'Come see us sometime.' He'd already given me the Laguna Beach address, his first visit. I didn't think much about the invitation to come down there because I thought he wanted to forget he and his boy had ever been separated."

"He must be a good actor."

She was silent, watching Sader with stubborn mistrustful eyes.

"Are you sure you didn't meet this young woman, Wanda Nevins? She was a good friend of Tina Champlain's."

"I don't think she ever came around her while she lived next to me."

"Tina Champlain might have mentioned the name."

"I don't remember it. I didn't meet any of her friends except Mr. Perrine and his father. It was as if she'd cut herself off from her old life, I thought. She'd made a clean break, she'd met Mr. Perrine afterward and he was about all she had."

"No relatives mentioned?"

"Not to me. That aunt was a big surprise."

"What about the little boy—some means of identification, scars and birthmarks, and so on?"

"He didn't have any. He had a perfect little body. Oh, he was getting sort of thin. He was a quiet child, soft-spoken, never in your way. But he never even had a cold, nor sniffles, during the time I knew them."

"The beach air must have agreed with him, then. He was sickly when she moved from West L.A."

Mrs. Cecil shook her head. "I wouldn't know about that. I moved in after Mrs. Champlain had lived there a while —several months at least."

Sader knew that he had another drive to Laguna ahead of him. He thanked Mrs. Cecil and took his leave.

CHAPTER NINE

Sader drove down the coast, fast. Dark had drawn in. The wind whined against the car. There were a few lights out at sea, pinpricks on the black, a couple of passing ships and a twinkling tower where they were drilling offshore for oil. When Sader got to Huntington Beach he pulled into a drive-in for coffee. He hadn't eaten since breakfast, still wasn't hungry. He felt nervous and full of an apprehension that had no focus. Mad, too. He had the sensation of having run through a bog, of the bog having attached itself to him, sucking underfoot.

He drank the coffee too fast and burned himself.

Two nights ago, his first meeting with old man Gibbings, the case had seemed straight as an arrow, not much more than a casual errand. Find a kid and let Gibbings know where he was. Like that.

Sader slapped fifty cents on the tray and honked his horn, though a sign on the side of the drive-in asked specifically that lights alone be blinked when one was ready to leave.

He sailed through Newport and Balboa, climbed the hill to Corona del Mar, sailed on southward toward Laguna. When the time came to turn, he almost overshot, had to brake fast, heard tires squeal behind him. A car skidded past, a profane voice drifting back to him. Sader drove up the hill to Wanda's house. He parked and crossed the court-yard, passing the raised bed—in it an Oriental garden light struck patterns on the papyrus and banana trees. He rang the bell. There was no sound of music from inside as before, and no one came to answer.

He knocked. The door sounded thick and secure under his knuckles. He tried to find a way to see inside, but the windows were small and high and opaque. They showed a reflected light, though. He went around the house, through the open space between it and the garage. The wind funneled in here, chilled with the smell and taste of the sea. He found a window, and it was one he could see through. Past a darkened alcove of some kind, probably a dining space, he could see a part of the living room. The big Buddha sat there counting his toes, there was the end of a shoji screen, a stack of cushions, but no sign of Wanda Nevins.

He went farther, found the door of the kitchen, tried the knob. It was locked. Past the door was another window, shoulder-high; Sader figured it must be the window above the sink, and he was pleased to see that inside the screen the pane was lifted. He was working on the screen when he heard a growl. He cupped his eyes, sticking his face against the screen, and inside in the dim dark he saw a four-legged shape and a double row of the finest dog teeth anywhere.

The dog was on the sink, looking at Sader and baring his fangs. Sader whistled softly and said, "Hey, Brucie, you remember me."

This must not have been Bruce. It didn't go away and the growls increased. Sader drew back, then jabbed a finger hard at the window and was rewarded by the sound of a businesslike *snap*.

"You want to be like that, it's okay with me," Sader said. He could see the brute's eyes gleaming in there like a pair of wet marbles.

He stepped over to the door. There was a faint thump, as the dog jumped off the sink. "You in there, baby?"

Baby growled to let him know.

"Tell Mama I'll be back."

He tried the doorbell one last time, a forlorn hope, and then went back to the car. He had the door open, one foot inside, when he decided to take a good look at the big house on the side of the hill across the street. The wide windows blazed with light. Probably it was designed to give a fine view of the sea, but it should give a fine view too of whatever went on over here. Provided the neighbors chose to look. Sader crossed the street and climbed about twenty-five stone steps, crossed a flagstone terrace and rang the bell.

A man with a red face, bald-headed, in his pants and undershirt and carrying a can of beer, opened the door and said, "Yeah?"

"I'm looking for Miss Nevins."

"She ain't here. Our name's Pickett. You got the wrong number, buddy."

A big television set was going full blast in the room, the corner away from the windows, and a woman was sitting facing it; she didn't even look around at Sader. "I know," Sader said, "she's your neighbor across the street. I thought you might know where she is tonight."

"We bought this place up here on this hill because it's private," said the bald-headed man. "We lived for more'n twenty years in Minneapolis, lived with my mother-in-law and my wife's brothers, and when we come out here we was ready to be alone. And we are. And we ain't prying and spying on nobody."

"Oh, it wasn't that—"

"You bet it wasn't. I don't even know her name."

Sader said desperately, "But you've seen her."

"She waved one morning and I didn't wave back. Like I said, we come here to have our own life, to ourselves. I couldn't tell you if she's a blonde or a redhead or what."

The door was closing. "Have you seen a child? A little boy?"

"Nope. Two dogs. Big ones. That's all." He jammed the door shut in Sader's face.

Sader drove on into Laguna, found a public phone booth at the edge of a parking lot, looked for the name of Nevins. Wanda was there, and that was all. No Mr. Nevins. Sader put in a dime and rang the number, just in case she was home now, but got no answer.

He went out, the bog clinging to his feet, and got into the car and sat there looking through the windshield at the main intersection of Laguna, the place where the canyon road met the coast highway, and all the spinning lights and

103

the dancing neon had their echoes behind his eyes; he was dizzy. "I don't believe it," he said out loud. "I don't believe the damned kid even exists." But then that didn't work either; he got to remembering what Mrs. Cecil had said about the sun-tanned man who had driven a red convertible and had taken Ricky Champlain away, probably with her waving a happy good-bye from the porch, and Sader wanted to beat his fist on the steering wheel.

He decided he must be hungry. He had a cheeseburger and a glass of milk and a cigarette, tried to relax. Tried to remember whatever it was he'd been doing when old man Gibbings had walked in. Probably something important, and they were losing clients and gaining a bad reputation by the minute because he wasn't attending to it. The carhop came and thanked him for the tip and took the tray away. As she walked into the light her legs shone like silk below the fluffy skirt, and Sader yawned, and then thought, My God, I really must be beat. I don't even want a second look. He rubbed his head.

He hated to drive back without having seen Wanda Nevins.

He tried to think back through that last talk he'd had with her, late in the office. She'd said, "You can admit, for instance, that the people who want to find the baby don't want to give him any money. They want *him*." And then Sader had craftily side-stepped by letting her know that it was old man Gibbings they were both talking about, and that there was nothing she could sell Gibbings but that if she wanted to let go of the information, the kid's whereabouts, he'd give her a hundred. It would go on the expense account, a nice short cut and cheap at the price he saw now; but she hadn't responded as he had thought she might.

In fact, she'd acted as if he had just popped a Roman candle in her face. And going to the door, that last crack: "Mr. Sader, you're working in the *dark*."

He answered her now: "I sure am, kiddo."

But what in the hell had she meant by it?

Turning in the seat to back from his slot beside the restaurant, Sader saw a white square in the back seat, and remembered the box of nothings he had found in the trash barrel at Tina's place. He made a promise to himself: first thing in the morning he'd hit *Betty's Baby Shop*.

He awoke in the middle of the night, again, and smoked, and stood at the window to stare at the lights and to listen to the jets. They were busy tonight, probably having some sort of tactical wingding, and the old house vibrated to their goings and comings. It wasn't raining, the night was clear, there was a look of peace about the empty dimlit streets and the far-off glow of the airfield, and Sader wished that some of the repose would invade his soul. He itched inwardly with a restless anger.

There was some whole item, like a screw loose in a crippled machine, that was fouling it all. He couldn't find it but he could sense it. He could sense the lack of orientation in himself, the failure to come to grips, the fumbling with chaos like a puzzle that didn't fit and wouldn't fit until the pieces that didn't belong had been tossed out. And what didn't belong? Where was the screw loose? "I'm damned if I know," he told the windowpane. "I'm full as hell of similes but I can't figure worth a hoot."

In the morning he rolled out and showered and shaved and dressed. He had a cup of coffee. He fed the parrot, who tried to take off a couple of fingers with an iron beak. The friendly setter wanted to jump up on him and lick his face. He managed to slobber on Sader's necktie, which had to be changed. Finally Sader got the pair all watered and fed, and left.

Betty's Baby Shop was north of Santa Monica, near the beach, and Sader drove by Tina's house on the way. The morning was cloudy and gray. The broken houses waiting to be moved looked inexpressibly lost and forgotten. Sader knew that there was nothing to see, nothing to be found, but whenever he looked at the place he was struck by the sudden change Tina seemed to have made in her life, coming here. Perhaps this was a part of the secret that eluded him. For some reason she had broken with her past, discarded old friends, rejected her church and its associations.

He didn't stop. He drove north, turned in at the smart shopping center which served this part of West L.A. *Betty's Baby Shop* had a sign shaped like a big white Teddy bear, and a slim woman in a white smock and imitation nurse's cap was taking down the CLOSED sign on the door.

He followed her in. She was in her fifties, gray-haired, very motherly in appearance. She smiled gently at him and Sader decided her teeth were her own, and that she was exactly the kind of woman who ought to sell baby stuff to young inexperienced mothers. He had the box under his arm. He laid it on the counter and took off the lid. She came to see, not disapproving or even surprised, and said, "Well, what have we here?"

"I was hoping that you could tell me."

She gave him a quick look, then picked up the lid to read the embossed lettering. She frowned over the cracked, spotted paper. "It's old. We don't use this box any more."

"What about the stuff inside?"

Again she gave him the quick, sizing-up look, trying to figure out what he was and what kind of crazy act he was pulling, perhaps. She put down the lid and carefully tilted the lower part of the box, using her left hand to urge the litter out upon the showcase. She found the tarnished locket and chain, laid it aside. The collection of ribbons she put far off, as if they amounted to little. She picked at the lace with a nail and said, "Irish." The stray buttons, the loose lavender, she left in the box. She picked up the baby's mitten, holding it in the fingers of both hands, and looked across it at Sader and nodded. "Is this what you wanted me to notice?"

"I really didn't have a plan. I'm just hoping for information. The woman this belonged to is dead, and her child has disappeared, perhaps taken away by relatives—we don't know."

Her eyes were thoughtful. "I remember her."

It caught him unprepared. "What?"

She put the mitten down where he could see it. "This is handmade. It was made by a lady, a very old lady, who used to knit and crochet for us. She was slow and her eyes were poor and she didn't make many of these sets. I might explain, this mitten was part of a pair, and it came with a matching bonnet and jacket. Probably you don't realize it, being a man—" The tone was patronizing but Sader didn't take time to resent it. "—but the work is exquisite."

"But you said you remembered the mother."

"I'm explaining why I remember her. This mitten isn't something you'd find in some dime store, it was made by hand and it was the only one of its pattern, it and its mate."

Sader felt sweat come out on his face, he was in such a hurry to have her start in on Tina Champlain. "Well . . . and so—"

He couldn't hurry her, she was sweetly thoughtful, and she was trying to treat him as she did the nervous, unsure, pregnant young women.

"I saw this knitted. You see, the lady who worked for us when she could, when she felt well enough, was my own mother."

Sader made some kind of sympathetic cluck; he knew now without her telling him that the old lady must be dead and that his bringing in the mitten had roused a host of memories.

"The baby was darling. See the pink touch here? She was the most beautiful little girl, tiny, not more than a couple of months at the most, and already she had golden hair, all curls, just like a doll's."

She was still standing there, a calm and friendly and motherly woman, and the little shop was the same one he had entered a few minutes before, there were baby clothes and all sorts of rattles and toys, strollers and rocking horses, the light was still distinct, but Sader had an enormous hollow soaring sensation, as if he'd just been elevated into the center of a thunderclap. He heard himself saying weakly, "You've made a mistake." And when she shook her head, he whispered, "Haven't you?"

"No."

Hell, Tina had bought the mitten for a gift, then, she'd brought in someone else's kid.

"I remember how proud she was, a new mother. Mrs.—wait a minute, I'll think of it. I keep thinking *lake*. Lake something."

"Champlain." He had never thought of the name in this connection.

"Yes, that's it. And you say she's dead now? I'm so sorry. Let's see, the baby would be about—" She paused to think. "—about five, now."

"Yes, he is."

"*She* is."

Sader was leaning on the counter, concentrating on the little mitten, trying to fight off the sensation of having lost all bearings in this affair.

"I surprised you, didn't I?" she asked.

"You sure did."

At the same time, other items were hammering to be remembered, among them the remark by Mrs. Cecil, something about being puzzled because of the baby things she'd seen in Tina's house, a remark he'd brushed over because he had such interest in the man who had come for the kid. Mrs. Cecil, being a woman, had realized that all of the baby things Tina had treasured were *girl*-baby things, and there

Ricky was, a boy. No wonder she'd suspected an adoption or some such. There were other details, too—Mrs. Bowen, in her wheel chair, beginning an explanation of the baby's illness with "*She was* . . . it had something to do with a heart defect." And most of all, Wanda Nevins streaking for the door with "Believe me, Mr. Sader, you're working in the *dark*."

He groaned, and the woman across the showcase patted his hand as if he might be beginning labor.

Hell, everybody in the whole damned business had been wise, but him. Sader wiped the sweat off his face and thought about old man Gibbings, and how Gibbings had been so careful to say he mustn't be identified as the baby's grandpa. Sader's hands knotted on the case as if he might have them around Gibbings' neck.

"Have I upset you?" she wondered in her soft comforting tone, as if people came in every day and got worked up over a baby's change in sex. "I wish I could give you some more information," she went on, "but Mrs. Champlain only came back a time or two, and she didn't bring the baby. In spite of its being such a cute little thing, a really beautiful little girl, it wasn't a strong child, there was something wrong with its heart."

"Yes, I've heard so."

Some of it was gradually growing clearer, and he was fighting off the sensation of having lost his way. He knew why Tina Champlain had made such an abrupt, mysterious change, moving from her home to a new neighborhood, giving up her church and its associations, discarding all old friends. The move must have coincided with the change in children.

Gibbings had tricked him, holding back a part of the truth. Gibbings had tricked himself more than anybody, Sader thought grimly, hamstringing the man who was working for him. You had to be damned stupid to pull it. Or you had to have a motive so stinking you couldn't risk even a private detective getting wind of it.

He thanked the woman behind the showcase, picked up the stuff and put it back in the box and headed for the door.

"When you're all through with that mitten—" she called after him.

"I'll mail it back to you," Sader promised.

CHAPTER TEN

The receptionist had been briefed; she jumped up as soon as she saw Sader and wriggled her way around the desk and said breathlessly, "Mr. Gibbings left word that you're to phone him at home tonight. He asked that you not come here again."

Sader put her firmly aside, noting during the slight tussle that certain parts of her were foam rubber and somewhat detachable. He opened the door to Gibbings' office and went in, shutting the door behind him. Gibbings sat over behind the desk, leaning forward, his face in shadow. He glanced up briefly.

Sader went to the desk and said, "Mr. Gibbings, this is the third day I've been working for you. I don't work cheap but I work hard, and the net result of your dough and my running around is that I know you're a goddam liar."

If he had thought Gibbings might show surprise, or guilt, some defensive reaction, he was wrong. Gibbings seemed embarrassed. He straightened a couple of papers on the desk and hooked a pen into its holder. "Sit down, please."

"You give me a line of bull now and I'll give you a swipe in the chops," Sader said, "even if you are as old as hell."

"Just sit down."

Sader went to a chair and dropped into it. His face and hands felt hot, and he was sweating. "You've played with my time and maybe with a kid's life. You're either some kind of a crook or you're crazy."

Still Gibbings didn't look worried or astonished; tired, more than anything. "I had hoped the job would be so simple that you'd find the child without running into any complications."

"What the hell motive do you have, hunting for this kid?" Sader almost shouted. "He isn't your grandchild!" When Gibbings did nothing except shrink back a little into his chair, Sader went on more calmly: "I'll tell you the only way it figures, the only way it makes sense. Your daughter is demanding the child she bore five years ago. And so in desperation you're trying to find Tina Champlain's orphan. But it isn't the same kid, and your daughter's going to know it. Even illegitimate mothers are told the sex of their babies. And your daughter gave birth to a girl."

Gibbings spread his hands on the desk. They were old and knotted, the veins big under the shriveled skin. The white mustache sagged like a bunch of wet feathers. "My daughter knows that she bore a girl and that the baby died when it was three years old. Can't you get it through your head at last, Sader, that all of this affair has nothing to do with her?"

Sader had taken out his wallet, had started to yank bills from it. But Gibbings said, "Don't throw my money at me until I tell you something more."

"I don't feel very patient."

"I can see that. But let's forget that I didn't outline the situation completely, and the reasons for it—I'll get to them later. Let's go back to the heart of the matter. The letter. The abominable thing that is happening to this child."

"It's a lie like the rest of it," Sader said with conviction.

"No. No, it isn't. The letter came by ordinary mail. I didn't concoct it. I believe in it. I think that the child Mrs. Champlain left after her death is being horribly abused. I want you to find him. You're for hire and that's the job I still want done."

Sader said, "You'd better get back to those reasons you just mentioned."

"Yes," Gibbings agreed in a voice like a croak. "To get back. I have a bad conscience. To put it simply, I revenged myself on someone and for quite a while I felt fine about it."

"You got back at the man your daughter loved," Sader said.

"I thought so. When I looked at the baby in the hospital I told myself that here was a tool for vengeance. He would have wanted that child if he had known it existed. Pusher and climber that he is. Not because he loved Kit . . . don't let your imagination build anything like a dream of love. He thought he would use Kit to get into this firm, and then he meant to use this firm to go higher. Much higher. But he would have liked to know that he had had a child by Kit Gibbings."

"You won that round."

"Yes, and after all, considering all the circumstances, there wasn't much else I could do."

"You could have let her keep her baby."

"Not in our circle, Mr. Sader."

"Does she have a circle now?"

The old man's bitter eyes lit up, and Sader knew he had probed a spot that hurt. "At the time I had no way of knowing that she was to become an invalid."

"You ran her life," Sader said. "She was the good, respectable spinster daughter you couldn't get along without. The faithful companion. The one to keep your name active in charities. The hostess for your circumspect hospitality. She was indispensable, and when you found out she was going to become an unmarried mother, I'll bet you tore the roof off. And as far as I'm concerned, if you got misery out of it you got just what you damned well deserved."

"As you say," Gibbings said stiffly, "I got what I deserved. But we are wandering far afield."

"Not much. And I've got plenty of time."

"This child may not have."

"Now you listen to me," Sader said. "I'm goddam tired of your lies. You're going to tell me what you really want with Tina's orphan or I don't play any more."

Gibbings actually looked puzzled and dismayed, and Sader thought what a good actor he was. "I can't really explain further. I feel that I owe Mrs. Champlain something, in some vague way. She loved my daughter's baby, she kept it during its short life. I want to help the child she took in after the baby died."

"Don't tell me that a horned toad of your age and disposition is taking up philanthropy."

Gibbings shook his head. "I shouldn't have come to you. There must be people more co-operative. Less belligerent."

"Do you mean to tell me that you're really on the level?"

Gibbings cleared his throat. "I am really, as you say, on the level."

They looked at each other in silence, the stony old man with the white mustache, the time-bitten face and the eyes like two steel balls, and the detective who was half-convinced and didn't want to be. Sader rubbed his hand across his head, where the short-cropped hair, once red and now thick with silver, sprang erect once his hand had passed. He regarded old man Gibbings with dislike. "I believe you mean it. What do you know about the little boy?"

"Nothing at all. I had a note from Mrs. Champlain when the baby died. She thought I might want to attend the funeral."

"Did you?"

"No. I sent a wreath."

"With Love from Grandpa?"

"That's not funny, Mr. Sader."

"It doesn't sound funny even to me," Sader said.

"The baby's death came a few months after Mr. Champlain had died in the plane crash. I imagine that Mrs. Champlain must have felt quite alone. I thought about offering her help, perhaps asking if she'd want a job here with us, or something like that, and then I decided against it. There was always the chance of some stray slip, some gossip getting a foothold."

"Oh, yes, you'd see it that way."

"Then I ran into this Wanda Nevins and she told me Mrs. Champlain had another child, a little boy about the age of the baby who had died."

"Why didn't you tell me this?" Sader demanded, his anger rising again.

"I thought you'd find the child without any trouble."

"Whoever took him away after Mrs. Champlain's death made a good job of covering his tracks. This is a description." Sader told Gibbings what Mrs. Cecil had related concerning the boy's so-called father, the youth and the virile appearance, and the sun-streaked hair and the tan. "He drove a red convertible. Does it sound like anyone you know?"

"It sounds like hundreds of young men I see driving the streets of Los Angeles every day," Gibbings muttered. "But no one I know."

"Probably he was a friend, a volunteer for the job. Or hired for it. I don't want to waste time trying to run him down on such a general description. We're going to have to find out where Mrs. Champlain got the boy. I suspect, through Wanda Nevins . . . in the same way she got your daughter's baby."

"I had thought so. That's why I sounded Wanda out before I called on you."

"And what did you really get from her?"

"Nothing. I didn't even dare ask directly about the child. She knew I had no reason to be interested in him. I made up a yarn about wanting to recover the papers having to do with the original adoption, asking where Mrs. Champlain's things had been stored. She asked me if I had read of the drowning in the papers—this was the first I'd heard of it, and I was wary. I kept expecting a trick of some sort. Finally she more or less told me that any information she had was for sale, and that's when I blew up, and hung up the phone."

No wonder, Sader thought, that Wanda had been astonished to find out from him that old man Gibbings was really looking for the child.

Sader said, "You've got a point, there—the house is totally empty. She must have had furnishings and personal belongings. I'll try to find out from Mrs. Cecil who has them now. I want to put an attorney on the job of running down a will, if it exists."

Gibbings moved impatiently in his chair. "I don't understand why you can't simply find the little boy and see what's happening to him."

"I can't find him because someone doesn't want him found."

Gibbings gave him a sharp glance. "You're supposed to be somewhat of an expert in finding missing persons."

Sader wondered who had given him such a good reputation. "There are a dozen good ways to trace an adult. They don't apply where a child is concerned."

Gibbings seemed to think about it. "Very well, put a lawyer on it."

"First of all, I'll go back to Wanda Nevins."

"You won't get anything out of her."

"This time, I think I might."

Sader took a long last look at Gibbings. Somewhere inside that hard-bitten tyrannical shell was a soft spot, a core of decency. Hard to believe, but he really had been touched by the plight of an unknown child. It was a revelation as startling as though Gibbings had suddenly sprouted wings.

Sader went to his car, got in, paused with his hand on the switch. It occurred to him then that in this case he was at a new beginning. He had been searching for Gibbings' grandchild, and it no longer existed. The child he wanted to find had a background and a history completely hidden.

There were people involved now of whom he knew nothing—the real parents of the little boy. The abuse of which the letter spoke could have its motive with these other people.

He remembered that the letter had been worded as if the writer believed Ricky to be the child adopted in infancy. This he couldn't understand at all.

Tina Champlain had made such a complete break in her life that no one had remained, except Wanda Nevins, of those who had known her while she had had the baby girl. So who was there to know the history of the original adoption? Gibbings was sure that Wanda had not written the letter. It was possible that Brent Perrine knew the truth about Ricky. Sader remembered the incident of the letter that Brent hadn't produced, the hint that he actually didn't wish to help Sader in the search. But Brent or his father wouldn't have written that letter to Gibbings. It had been a woman's letter—on this point Sader was positive—with a woman's sentimental and indignant attitude over the wrongs practiced on the boy. The woman believed—or for some reason was pretending to believe—that Ricky and the baby adopted at birth were one and the same.

If it was pretense on her part, what in hell was the motive behind it?

Sader crushed out his cigarette and started the motor, pulled away from the curb, still thinking about it.

The clouds broke and drifted away as he drove south. The sun came out. It was just past eleven when he reached the outskirts of Laguna, the brightest hour of the morning. He turned up the hill to Wanda's place. The light off the sea was glassy. He parked, and walked through the courtyard, paused at the door to look back. The Oriental lantern still showed a light, there amidst the foliage; and then he noted that the light over the door was burning, too.

Wanda hadn't come home during the night, then.

He went around to the kitchen and looked in at the window over the sink. He could see a big daffodil-yellow range and refrigerator, a lot of cupboards; but the dog wasn't there to show his teeth. Sader whistled in through the screen, and then listened, but there was no answering tap of toenails on the linoleum. He rattled the doorknob, and there was still no answer.

He looked around. Here in the breezeway he was out of sight of the neighbors. The slopes below had houses, and there was the traffic artery, but Sader decided to take the risk. "Here's where I lose the seat of my pants, probably." He took out a knife and jimmied the catch of the screen above the sink.

Once inside, he crouched against the opened window and waited, fully expecting a big brown hunk of muscle and fangs to come running. When the house remained still, empty-sounding, he got down off the sink board and went into the dining alcove. The lights were burning in the living room beyond. The draperies were pulled, shutting out the sun; it looked much as he had glimpsed it on the night before.

He crossed in front of the big Buddha, wondering as usual what quirk of mood, or what desire to be different, had made Wanda want it.

The fireplace gave forth a miasma of ash, though there was little in it except some smudges on the clean brick. It looked to Sader as if something no bigger than a couple of sheets of writing paper had been burned between the andirons, then crushed into the hearth. He went on into the hall. Here was unexpected brightness. At the end of the hall a window swung open, screenless, giving a view of the sea below. The sea wind swept in, bringing a smell of salt air, a touch of cold. For some reason Sader felt immensely lonely at that moment. The house seemed dead, and he was quite alone in it.

He opened the nearest door and there was the dog, perhaps the same dog that had snapped at him last night through the window. The dog was stretched out on a fluffy orange-colored bath mat and he was fine all the way from the tip of his tail to his collar. Something was wrong with his head. There was a bloody depression in the skull between his ears, and blood had run out upon the orange mat and even to the tiled floor.

Sader bent over him. The dog's head seemed to have been crushed by one heavy blow. As far as Sader could judge, it had happened right here. There was no indication the dog had been dragged injured or dying into the bathroom. Sader glanced into the shower cubicle, but it was clean and empty. He went back to the hall, but now he took out a handkerchief and wiped his prints off the knob of the bathroom door.

He used the handkerchief to wrap the next doorknob he touched. He found himself in a kind of studio, a dabbler's playroom. Here was a typewriter and a lot of paper on a desk, some books on how to become a writer, and across the room was a weaving loom, and next to it was an easel with a clean canvas in it. On a tiny table lay an array of oil paints. Pinned to the wall was a big astrological chart. An open window looked out in the same direction as the one in the hall, filling the room with sea glitter, and Sader felt that he had intruded into a place Wanda Nevins would never have wanted him to see.

"She tried everything," he said to himself, looking at it, remembering too the big Buddha that must be the souvenir of an excursion into Oriental philosophy. She had searched for herself here in this house, trying this and that, spending time and money in the search. He wondered what she had finally discovered.

He backed out, leaving the door ajar, turned to another door near the end of the hall.

She was in there.

The bed was big and low, covered with a white satin spread. A light burned in a bracket on the wall. The windows were covered by white satin draperies. A big mirror over the dressing table reflected Sader's figure as he walked forward.

It was a beautiful room, but Wanda didn't match it. She had died hard, died fighting. She lay with her head hanging over the edge of the bed, and Sader took one good look at her, making sure of the fact of death, and then he didn't look at her again.

CHAPTER ELEVEN

He went into the living room and sat down on a chair and smoked a cigarette. There was some thinking to be done, a course of action to be planned. Some legal angles had to be considered, relating to his hanging onto his license.

He wondered who represented the law on this particular hillside. The County Sheriff, probably, since it was north of the Laguna Beach city limits. He was certainly obligated, under the rules of his license, to co-operate with the Sheriff's office in reporting the murder of Wanda Nevins.

He had also a duty to a client, in this case old man Gibbings whom he found completely detestable. There was no way on earth, once the murder had been reported, to keep Gibbings' name out of it. The newspapers would seize on him like a pack of wolves. The tissue of secrecy would be torn. But it wasn't old man Gibbings that Sader found himself worrying about. He was remembering an elephant of a woman in red pants and green jersey blouse, with a painted face, who had described for him the only image he had of Kit Gibbings, sitting alone at a table at Hollywood Park and studying a racing form.

And it was somehow this woman he had never met, with her nice white gloves and her pot of tea, and her fifty-dollar hat that she didn't know was all wrong for her, it was this woman who slowly but surely tipped the scales for Sader.

He got off the chair, disposed of the cigarette butt in the bathroom, then went through the house swiftly. He found, in the hollow shell of the Buddha's backside, a locked steel box to which there seemed to be no key. He carried it into the kitchen, pried up the lid with a screwdriver.

It was empty. Someone who had had a key had beat him to it. He wiped his prints off the steel surface, left it on the sink.

In a hatbox on the top shelf of Wanda's closet were some bankbooks, bank statements, and a sheaf of canceled checks snapped together with a rubber band. Sader laid the checks on the dressing table and separated them with a pencil tip. They represented mortgage and house utility payments, and checks drawn for cash. The bankbooks had been issued by two different banks, one in Laguna Beach and one in Los Angeles. The Los Angeles account showed a savings account balance of a little more than twenty-two thousand dollars. The Laguna Beach account was a small checking operation; it appeared from what Sader could figure that four or five hundred dollars had been withdrawn every few weeks from the savings account in L.A. and deposited in the Laguna Beach account to make the mortgage and other payments.

The L.A. account had been started almost two years before with a single deposit of forty thousand dollars.

Sader put the bankbooks and the checks back in the box, taking care not to leave prints, and returned the box to its shelf. He looked around for Wanda's purse, found it on the dressing table, a big calfskin bag. Inside was a wallet, a new checkbook, and the usual cosmetics. In the wallet identification section were Wanda's driver's license and a charge card for an oil company. There were five ten-dollar bills and some loose change. The new checkbook showed no entries.

Passing again through the living room, Sader paused at the fireplace. Something had been burned there, all right. A sheet or two of writing paper, perhaps. He noted that there was nothing else out of the ordinary to be noted. No disorder; Wanda hadn't fought for her life here. She had been attacked and destroyed in the bedroom. The dog had been killed in the bathroom.

One dog was missing.

Sader removed his prints from the inner surfaces of the window, and from the sink board. Then he let himself out of the kitchen door, crossed the breezeway to a door that opened into Wanda's garage. Inside in the gloom was a small blue sports car of foreign make, nothing remarkable about it except that in the glove compartment was a fifth of vodka, about half-full, a couple of paper cups with moisture in the bottoms.

The only things stored here besides the car were some gardening tools, practically new, and some sacks of fertilizer. Sader stepped back into the breezeway, walked to his car, got into it and drove away slowly, trying to look as ordinary as possible. There were no faces in the windows of the house directly above. As far as he could tell, no one was paying any attention to him at all. It was a matter on which he simply had to take a chance, anyway.

The neighbor up there, with his passion for privacy, might or might not remember for the police that a man had come inquiring if Miss Nevins had had a little boy about. It was remarkable to Sader what perverse tricks casual memory could play.

As he drove, he forced himself to reconsider the circumstances of Wanda's death. Her clothes had been badly mauled, but she had been fully dressed when she had died. Nothing like the little tan sunsuit in which he had first seen her. She had had on a deep-green street dress. Torn at the neck, the sleeves ripped from the shoulders; but when it had been entire, the sort of dress she would have worn to go into the city.

She'd had on sheer hose, high-heeled black pumps. Something nagged at this point, and then he remembered the calfskin bag. Wrong color. She wouldn't have carried it wearing the black pumps, so it meant that the killer had caught her in the process of changing, that she hadn't as yet transferred her personal clutter to whatever purse matched the shoes.

Some time last night she had come home, had changed to go out again. Someone had ridden with her, sharing the vodka from the paper cups.

An excuse had been made, the dog taken into the bathroom, to be disposed of with a single, silent blow. Then, leisurely perhaps, the murderer's attention had been turned to the girl. She may have screamed once or twice—there were no near neighbors. The beating and general destruction must have taken some strength, and here Sader found himself thinking about the young husky type who had taken away Tina's little boy.

You could kill without that kind of brutality. Sader remembered his feeling that the young man had been hired, someone to act the part of a father; and for the first time he felt unsure of his hunch. The treatment described in the letter, the abuse practiced on the child, had the smack of what had been done to Wanda Nevins.

Sader found himself glancing at his own hands on the wheel, wondering what had turned them so cold.

He had no proof at all, and yet he was convinced that Wanda Nevins had been a blackmailer and that she had died in the practice of her job.

When he got into Newport Beach he found a public phone booth and called Gibbings' office. The receptionist was stilted and cool, and told him Mr. Gibbings had gone to lunch. It might have been the truth. He couldn't get anything else out of her. From the same phone booth he called the Sheriff's office and reported, anonymously, the death of Miss Nevins and the address of her home.

From his office in Long Beach he called his attorney friend. "You've been engaged by Hale Gibbings to check up on a will. This involves the estate of a woman named Tina Champlain who drowned about six months ago at Catalina."

"Look, my God, you called me a couple of nights ago and I've already done a little checking and so far—"

"You have been engaged by Mr. Gibbings to act as his attorney in this affair."

"Oh. It's become an affair, has it?"

"Mr. Gibbings was a friend of Mrs. Champlain's. He decided to check up and make sure that her child was being cared for, and that he had inherited her estate, and so forth. I've been working for you on these angles."

"You have?" The lawyer's tone was full of dry amusement.

"It's the best I can do," Sader said. "I want a once-remove from Gibbings and this will have to serve." It wouldn't serve long, he reminded himself, if the cops went to work on Gibbings' receptionist. She'd soon set them straight on who'd been storming in to see the old man.

"You mean you're trying to keep your client's name out of something nasty," the lawyer said, "and I'm going to be the buffer." He waited for Sader to say something. "Can't you let me know what I'm sticking my neck out for?"

"If you don't know it won't worry you. Just keep on looking for some trace of Mrs. Champlain's estate. Concentrate on that flight insurance."

"Let me know when you want out of jail."

"I'll do that."

Sader settled himself to wait. If there was a lead from Wanda Nevins to him, either through an identification of his car by a neighbor, or through some remark made to someone by Wanda before her death, or through some memo in the house that he hadn't located, he should be hearing about it pretty quickly. Otherwise he might be contacted days from now as the cops worked their way out into the fringes of possibilities, say through the Perrines—or perhaps never.

At five o'clock he phoned Gibbings' office again and was told that Mr. Gibbings had left for the day.

The homes that faced each other across the lawns of Tiffany Square were Victorian monstrosities, mostly vine-covered brick. They had cost money, and they were old. The square was shut in with an ornate steel fence anchored to stone pillars. It was all very quiet, remote, and when Sader thought of living in it he was glad of some of the wilder portions of his youth.

The Gibbings home occupied a corner of the square. The walk was mossy and the door overhung with vines. You pulled a handle in the middle of the door and the bell clanged right inside. Remembering the pebbled aluminum and orange glass of the Wilshire Boulevard offices, Sader decided that this house in Tiffany Square was where Gibbings really enjoyed himself.

An ancient maid in black cotton and white organdy apron came to the door. She listened while Sader explained that he must see Mr. Gibbings right away. She said that she would see if Mr. Gibbings was in. She shut the door, having no illusions about Sader's status in life.

Gibbings himself came back. He didn't look angry or put out because his hired man had invaded Tiffany Square. Sader thought he looked haunted. "Come in. This way. That's all, Irene."

Irene peered critically at a hall table Sader was passing at the moment, as if he might be breathing dust onto it, and then removed herself. Sader followed old man Gibbings into a furnished mausoleum of a room, vast and shadowy. A small fire glowed in the enormous grate—just for looks; the place was warm to the point of mugginess. Gibbings indicated a chair for Sader and sat down facing it. "You've come here because Wanda has been murdered?"

Sader had the feeling that sand had begun to slide under his feet. "How did you hear about it?"

"The Sheriff's office called me. They wanted to know when I had last seen her, and when I told them it had been several years, and that recently I had only contacted her by phone, they didn't seem to believe it."

"They told you then that she was dead?"

"I asked what had happened to her, and they said she'd been murdered. They expected some reaction, I think. A lot of protests, my saying I didn't do it. All I did . . . I said I hadn't known Miss Nevins well but that I wished them luck in finding her killer."

"What led them to you?"

The haunted expression deepened in Gibbings' face. "I didn't ask. I suppose, because I knew somehow that something like this was inevitable. It was inevitable from the moment I knocked on your office door."

Sader was thinking of the effort he had made, the cover he had provided through the lawyer, and all for nothing now.

Gibbings' tone took on a dragging note. "It happened because you, Mr. Sader, are a bungler. You are inept. I provided you with a simple task and you preferred to complicate it.

You wished to involve my daughter, though she had no connection with it, and you apparently ran through the people surrounding Mrs. Champlain during her life . . . anyone with whom she'd had the least contact . . . without turning up any sort of a clue. It should be a simple matter to find a child, sir. He is a living organism, he's not a piece of wood you can stick into a box and keep out of sight indefinitely. He has to eat and sleep and play and unless he's been stuck in a cellar and forgotten and has died, there must be people who see him every day. And those people should be discoverable."

A bit of burning wood popped in the grate. Sader ran a finger around inside his collar.

"I'm not accusing you of trying to shake me down," old man Gibbings said. "You're not in Miss Nevins' class at all. Not clever enough. You're just stupid and bungling."

"Thanks," said Sader grimly.

"You can give me my money back now, if you've a mind," Gibbings offered.

Sader looked at him, at the white mustache and the steel-colored eyes, the hunched posture like a hawk's, and shook his head. "I never was working for you, Mr. Gibbings. I didn't know it until a moment ago."

"And who, then—"

"I've been working for your daughter."

Two triangles of angry color blotched the skin under Gibbings' pouched eyes. "You are insolent, sir."

"I don't mean to be. I'm as sincere as hell. I don't know your daughter but I like her, Mr. Gibbings. She must be a lady in the best sense of the word. She's got guts. It would take guts to live here with you and to see her own youth die away, and to have one little slip and to pay like hell and then to become an invalid, still shut up here. And not to become a well-known wheel-chair drunk in all the best bistros. And not to take an overdose of pills, or shoot herself."

Gibbings was looking around in fury, and if there'd been something handy Sader knew he would have thrown it.

Sader rose from the chair. "I'm going to keep on working —for Kit Gibbings. Being the kind of woman she is, she'd want a thorough check made on Mrs. Champlain's little boy. When I'm finished I'll send the bill to your office."

Gibbings sprang from his own chair with an effect of being catapulted and careened toward Sader with a fist upraised. Sader hated to hit him. It was like knocking a dried twig off a rotten tree, but he struck down the arm and then pushed Gibbings bodily back into the chair. The old man sat there staring at the arm Sader had hit as if it might be broken. Sader bent over him, yanked at the claw-shaped hand. The skin was dry and cold but all of the finger moved like knives.

"You're okay."

"Get out!"

"Just going anyway."

The ancient maid was lurking under the stairs. She hurried after Sader, and outside on the brick step he heard the lock turn behind him. No flies on Irene. He had no doubt she'd heard every word.

He looked back at Tiffany Square from the big iron gateway. Against the dying light the chimneys were tall and black, the gables and turrets had the look of medieval grandeur. He waited for a couple of bats to sail out into the twilight and complete the sorcery, but nothing happened. Nothing ever would happen in Tiffany Square, on the surface. It and the people in it would be here unchanged fifty years from now, unless somebody planned a freeway through it and sent the bulldozers.

Sader stopped at a drive-in eatery on the way back to Long Beach, and sitting under the neon in his car he searched through what he had done, trying to find a thread in it that would lead him on. The murder of Wanda Nevins cast a light on things, a light he didn't like. Tina Champlain had found one child through the Nevins woman. It seemed logical she may have found the second, also. Had she paid forty thousand dollars for him? It didn't sound likely.

There had been something wrong about Mrs. Champlain's taking the little boy. She had hidden herself and him away. Wanda Nevins must have known a lot about it, and she hadn't told Sader because Sader hadn't asked the right questions nor offered the proper sums of cash. And now Wanda was dead, and he knew the kind of questions to ask—too late.

He looked at the food on his tray, finding it tasteless. Not because of Wanda. She had been a cool and clever woman who had used her wits to buy luxury and leisure, and her bargaining had brought her where she was now, on a coroner's slab. The thing that turned Sader's taste for food was still the thought of the child, the one who was whipped and who didn't get enough to eat.

When the car-hop had taken the tray Sader turned into the traffic. At the next intersection he swung west, toward Wilmington. It was a good time to see what the Perrines were doing.

CHAPTER TWELVE

The broken fence made a pale crosshatch against the dark.
Sader eased in through the gate, went up the uneven walk
to the porch, stood there in darkness and silence for a couple of minutes. Then he went around the house to the rear,
avoiding the clutter in the yard. There was a lot of reflected light from the sky, and he could see the boat hulls
on their chocks, and could smell the paint. At the rear door
he tried the knob, and the door opened.

He went in. There was a strong odor of spilled wine in
the kitchen, a concentration of almost etherlike strength.
Sader had brought a pencil-sized flashlight, used it now
to examine the room. At first the mess seemed only a little more disorganized, the beer cans shoved off onto the
floor and a chair smashed, and then Sader saw where the
wine had smashed, and decided that the two men had had
a fight. Then a prickle of warning brushed him, and he
clicked off the light and listened.

There had been some kind of noise from upstairs, too
vague to be identified. Sader used the light to guide himself

through the hall and up the stairs to the point where they turned, the spot where Brent Perrine had stood to reread the letter and to change his mind about showing it to Sader. He paused here again and heard the noise, a heavy breathless grunt. He went the rest of the way with caution. In the dark of the upper hall he waited, locating the sound of labored breathing.

He found old man Perrine with the light, and when he saw what had happened to him, Sader switched on the bedroom lamp.

Ralph Perrine lay across a patchwork quilt. It and a bare pillow and Perrine himself were the only things on the bare mattress. Sader thought to himself that Perrine must have been sick and the bed stripped because of it.

Perrine was stretched on his back, dressed only in a pair of shorts and his socks. His eyes gleamed up at Sader, but the expression was glazed and disoriented. The skin over the right temple was shiny and purple, bulging over a lump, and Sader could see where blood had run from his puffed lips. There were bruises on his body, several big ones along his ribs, as if he might have been kicked when he had fallen. In contrast to his tanned, seamed face and leathery arms and hands, the flesh of his body was white and doughlike.

Sader went out into the hall and located the bathroom. Some towels hung on a rack, several wadded and soiled ones and a couple by themselves that were neat and fresh. Sader thought, those clean ones belong to his son. He yanked a clean towel off the rack and ran cold water over one end of it, wrung it out, went back to the old man. He bent over Ralph Perrine and bathed the swollen face. The old man drew a couple of deep, shuddering breaths and a look of recognition came into his eyes.

"Somebody gave you a rough time. How long have you been lying here?"

Ralph's head turned, and he seemed to examine the room beyond Sader. Then he shut his eyes. "I need a drink. God's sake, get me one."

"Where do you keep the bottle?"

"Under the . . . No, he broke that. Wait a minute. In the closet, an old Army duffel bag—" He tried to lift himself on an elbow, and a look of astonished pain flattened his mouth and drew back the corners of his eyes.

"Don't try to sit up." Sader went to the closet, found the duffel bag on a hook. Inside, wrapped in a pair of old khaki pants, was a quart of muscatel. He brought it to the bed, broke the seal and unscrewed the cap, held it out to Ralph Perrine. The old man got himself up on an elbow. In spite of Sader's help, he trembled so that he could hardly drink. Some of the wine spilled. Sader looked around for a window.

When he had the window up he came back to the bed. Perrine held the bottle upright, shaking his head over it. He was making an obvious effort to keep the drink down. Sader handed him the damp end of the towel, and Perrine mopped his face gratefully. Sader sat down on the edge of the bed.

"Who worked you over?"

"It wasn't nothing. Just, me and Brent had a little argument."

"He played rough."

"I learned him to. Never wanted no pantywaist kid. This town, this part of it, a kid has to look after hisself. I learned him to use his fists and to ask questions afterward."

"How long since he left the house tonight?"

Perrine squinted at a clock on the bureau. The clock had run down, no longer ticked. "How would I know? I've been asleep."

"He helped you get to bed?"

Ralph Perrine tried to grin, but the grin went lopsided because of the lumps and bruises on his face. "Sure."

"When I left here yesterday it sounded as if a chair hit the wall in the kitchen. Was that when the fight started?"

"Well, I guess so." Perrine's wits were fuzzy; he was trying to keep a guard up against Sader's questions, and Sader could see the effort it took. "When I tried to iodine him, it kind of made him mad."

"I sort of got the idea he thought you were the one who took a shot at him."

"Heh, heh, heh," Perrine chuckled, pretending Sader had made a joke. "Now where'd you get a goofy idea like that?"

"It seemed to me that the direction the bullet came from was the house."

"Oh? Funny." He was stalling. He took another swig of wine and sweat stood out on the purple swellings. "Say, not to, uh, change the subject, or anything, but how're you coming along, finding Tina's kid?"

"I haven't found him. I know a little more about him. He wasn't the first baby she had adopted. Did you know it?"

The results of the beating Perrine had taken made an effective mask, hiding any sign of surprise. "I didn't know it. Well, I didn't pay much attention to the little kid. Brent and her used to talk about him, whether Brent might adopt him after they were married."

"Did Brent ever act jealous over the little boy?"

"Hee, hee, hee."

"No, I mean it. I'm asking a serious question. It wouldn't be the first time a man has resented a kid being around when he wanted to make love to the mother."

Suddenly Perrine seemed quite indignant. "Of course he wasn't jealous. What was there to be jealous about? He was a nice quiet little kid, what I saw of him. He was no trouble to nobody."

"Tell me this. Did she ever say anything about Ricky's real parents?"

Perrine squinted with elaborate thoughtfulness at the light. "I don't believe she did."

"Did she ever talk about how she happened to find him, why she adopted him?"

"All she ever said to me was, 'He belongs here with me.' I remember that. It was once when Brent asked her if she'd thought about putting the boy in military school."

"He was kind of young for plans like that."

"Oh, Brent was just passing time, you might say."

"Where do *you* think the boy is now?"

Something cunning and yet confused glimmered in the old man's eyes, an evil knowledge not yet complete. "Hell, I guess her folks must have him. It seems likely." In that moment Sader almost hit him.

It took a moment of iron self-control. Sader turned deliberately so that he wouldn't have to look at the old man. He stood up and walked to the window, and as he stood there he caught the sound of a motor below, and then the beam of headlights cut across the yard. Brent was home.

Sader sat down again on the edge of the bed.

The old man took another swallow of wine. He'd put away over a third of the bottle, and Sader thought that his breathing seemed heavier, that he was flushed. Suddenly Ralph Perrine lifted his head higher. "You know what? You know something about that little kid, that Ricky? He sure as hell looked like her a lot. Yessir."

Sader tried to figure out what could account for the switch. The old man seemed genuinely amused, his attitude was that of discussing an odd fact which had no bearing on anything important.

"He looked like Mrs. Champlain?" Sader said.

"I was surprised as hell when Brent told me he was adopted."

The back door slammed and there were footsteps downstairs. Sader watched the bedroom door.

"I thought, maybe she got him from a relative, maybe some girl in her own family got into trouble, and that would account for the resemblance." The old man nodded and grimaced over the wine.

"It's an idea." Sader was wondering if there might be some truth in it. Wouldn't something like this account for the aunt's rejection of the little boy?

There were footsteps in the hall below. They paused for a few moments, and Sader wondered if Brent had heard his father's voice and realized that someone must be up here with him. But when the steps resumed they were unhurried; they came up the stairs deliberately, casually, and then Brent was at the door looking in, lighted by the light from the lamp.

He wore a gray silk sport shirt and the usual denim pants, and filled both with the muscular tautness Sader remembered, and Sader thought again how much Brent personified the strong-man ads in the magazines of his youth, and how Brent even wore the strong man's expression of looking out over other people's heads as if seeking a proper opponent.

Brent said, "I'll be damned. I sure didn't think you'd be around again. I thought you'd be running."

"From what?"

"The cops. Don't you scare easy?"

"Not very. Why should I be running from cops?"

"Because Wanda Nevins was found murdered and you were seen down there about the time she must have died."

Sader got up and moved to where he could see Brent a little better in the lamplight. "Who identified me?"

"I don't know." Brent came to the doorsill and examined his father on the bed. Old man Perrine had lain down flat, the wine bottle concealed under a fold of the quilt. He was pretending to be asleep. "The county cops called me and I drove down to Santa Ana and talked with a lieutenant there. He seemed to know all about old man Gibbings and you, and what you wanted from Wanda . . . the whereabouts of Tina's boy."

"Somebody put in a damned quick word," Sader commented. "What strikes me is that the cops must know I have an office with a phone in it, and if they want me, why haven't they called?"

Brent shrugged, went to the end of the bed and bent there staring at his father. "Hey! He must have fallen down the stairs."

"He said you and he had a little argument."

"He's a liar," Brent responded, either in quick anger or an excellent imitation of it. "When I left him here this morning he was passed out on the bed, fit as a fiddle."

"Maybe his bruises just hadn't had time to swell," Sader suggested. He noted that Brent's hands on the metal bed frame had no marks on them, no scars on the knuckles, and he didn't see how the son could have beaten the old man—barehanded, anyway—without having a few marks to show for it.

"I wouldn't do that to him. Hell, he's my old man," Brent said, giving Sader a hard glance.

"About Wanda Nevins— Did she ever talk to you about her source of income, how she made her living, what she worked at?"

Brent hesitated, then answered, "I told you before . . . remember? I told you I'd only met her a couple of times, and all I know about her was what Tina told me. She'd been in a jam, some kind of juvenile delinquency rap, and Tina had helped her out. They stayed friends."

"Do you think Tina Champlain ever gave her any money?"

Brent moved away from the end of the bed. He took out a pack of cigarettes, matches, lighted a cigarette and put the pack back in his pants' pocket. "Hell, no. Wanda had money. You could see it in her clothes, the way she acted and the way she took care of herself. Her car. Those damned dogs. They're purebred, they cost her plenty. She never needed anything of Tina's."

"Wait a minute. You said she came here asking about Tina's will, thinking Mrs. Champlain might have left her something."

"I said she never *needed* money. Not that she wouldn't *take* it. My God, if Tina had left a will and left her anything, she'd have snapped it up like a shark." Brent blew smoke out into the air above the prone figure of the old man. Sader had the feeling that behind the swollen lids, old man Perrine was watching his son. "What are you doing here tonight? Hiding out?"

It was a silly question. The Perrines were no friends of his and Brent knew that Sader knew it. "I'm here on the same business as before. Looking for the kid. I know he wasn't the first one Mrs. Champlain had adopted. It took a while to find that out."

Brent went on smoking.

Sader said, "Surely she had told you about the other baby."

"I just figured it wasn't any of your damned business," Brent replied.

"The aunt told me that Tina Champlain didn't have any right to the little boy."

"She always had a lot of trouble from that aunt," Brent

said. "And then maybe all the relatives were sore because there wasn't any money, the kid inherited what they thought they'd get."

"How do you know he inherited it?" Sader demanded. "I can't even find a trace of him."

"Well, of course, he must have inherited it," Brent said, his stare growing antagonistic.

"Not if he wasn't legally adopted. Not if Tina Champlain had simply taken him in to replace the child that had died."

Brent made an angry, dismissing gesture with the hand holding the cigarette. "Look, I don't know anything about it. And right now I want to get to work on my old man. He ought to have some liniment on those bumps. Someday he's going to break his neck, trying to get downstairs to the wine when he's already had too much." Brent moved over to bend above the old man. "Just look at him. An old soak. Dirty. The bed filthy. I can't keep the house in any order at all, he's always reeling through in his stinking clothes, falling over everything."

Sader decided that Brent was explaining the disorder of the kitchen, in case he had seen it.

"He was pretty positive that you and he had had a fight."

"D.t.'s . . . he imagines all kinds of things," Brent said angrily. He put a big hand on the old man's shoulder and shook hard, and the old man's good eye came open in a malevolent glare.

Sader went out of the room and down the stairs. He was tired of watching the play-acting, or whatever it was, that went on between the Perrines. He wondered in passing if Tina Champlain had ever come here, and what she had thought of the house. For some reason, it seemed to Sader that Brent Perrine was putting up with the mess in the manner one puts up with a temporary discomfort.

It didn't help him in what he had to do, to find Tina Champlain's orphan.

He drove back to Long Beach, parked, went upstairs to his office. He was fitting a key to the lock when he felt the approach of someone behind him in the dimly lighted hall. He looked back. The face and big frame was familiar. "Hello, Jackson."

"Got a minute, Sader?"

"Hell, I've got all night."

The Orange County man followed him in through the outer office to the room with the desks and the couch. He sat down on the couch and put his hat beside him. Sader went to his desk.

If it had been any other man from the Sheriff's office, Sader would have fought like a tiger over every scrap of information. But he knew Jackson, he had worked with him. He wasn't an ordinary cop. Jackson had intelligence and judgment, and what was more rare and more important, a sense of compassion. The years of working with the dregs hadn't blinded him to the face of humanity.

Sader began to talk. He outlined the case from its beginning in this room. He told Jackson how he'd found Wanda's dead body, and why he had cleared out and made an anonymous phone call. He wound up by explaining where he stood now, canned by old man Gibbings and determined to go on, on his own.

Jackson had lighted his pipe. He took it out of his mouth to say mildly, "I thought you worked for money."

"So did I," Sader admitted.

"So what's in it for you if you find the kid?" When Sader shrugged, Jackson went on, "Don't you see now that you can let us look for the kid without dragging in Miss Gibbings? She wasn't the mother. It's just a case of finding a little boy who didn't belong to anybody."

Sader winced.

"Incidentally," Jackson added, "there were two anonymous calls. Yours and another. About two minutes apart. I don't know which one came in first. They both reported the death. One of them said we'd better find out something about Mr. Gibbings and a man he had working for him, a private detective named Sader."

"That other call was from Wanda's murderer," Sader said slowly.

"It would seem so," Jackson agreed.

CHAPTER THIRTEEN

"I can't understand why you didn't get hold of me right away," Sader told Jackson.

"Just because somebody squawks, I don't have to jump. Not the way he wants me to jump, at least. I did some work on it before I came to you. I know you—something he didn't know."

"I hope you don't overlook the fact that he also knew of Gibbings' search for the boy, and my part in it."

Jackson nodded. "He could have found it out from Wanda Nevins. We figure they spent some time in the house before the murder."

"They left the vodka in the car."

"She wasn't ordinarily a vodka drinker. There was a case of expensive Scotch in one of the kitchen cupboards, a couple of bottles she'd worked on in the refrigerator." Jackson puffed on the pipe. "You think your business with Gibbings had something to do with her murder?"

"It's tied in somewhere," Sader said with conviction. "She had an angle and she was working on it. At first she thought she could play along with me, use me. And then she found out I was way off the beam. I was struggling along under the impression that the baby I had to find was old man Gibbings' grandson. That queered it for her, somehow. But then she knew that the kid had disappeared and that somebody was keeping him hidden. It was all she needed."

Jackson nodded behind the pipe. He was a big man, and gave the impression of judicial considering. "What about this pair you saw tonight, the Perrines?"

"So far, the only connection seems to be that Mrs. Champlain was in love with Brent and intended to marry him. And that she drowned off their boat at Catalina. The aunt seemed to think that Mrs. Champlain had loaned Brent some money for his boat business, but she's the only one who mentioned it. The old man said that if Tina had lived, his son would have gotten help from her, that the drowning had spoiled a lot of plans for them."

Jackson said, "You haven't traced any money?"

"Not yet. I have an attorney looking into the possibility of a will. The money—if there was any—and the little boy seem to have dropped out of sight together."

Jackson rose. "We'll find them. Meanwhile, if anything comes in from what you've done, let us know. You don't have to worry about any publicity for Miss Gibbings . . . well, you'd know that."

"I knew it," Sader said.

They understood each other. Sader wondered if Jackson's superiors had had the inspiration to send him, or whether Jackson had volunteered. In either case, it had been the only way they'd have gotten his co-operation.

"I'll run a make on the Perrines," Jackson said in parting.

Sader nodded, but he had a hunch neither the old man nor the son had any record, unless the old man had collected a few drunk arrests. Brent Perrine wasn't just physically fit. He was the kind of man who kept his private affairs in good order, too. Sader wondered in passing how Brent stood the old man's drunken disorder; and was struck again by his original conviction, that the old man had shot at his son from the house and that Brent had beaten his father thoroughly in retaliation. And again, seeing and sensing a corner of Brent's real nature, he guessed that keeping the score even would be a part of Brent's sense of the fitness of things.

Jackson let himself out of the office and Sader turned to the phone. There was no answer to his ring in the attorney's office. Sader locked up and went to his temporary home, and to bed.

In the middle of the night the dog wanted out. As soon as Sader went down and turned on the kitchen light, the parrot stirred and screeched and began to eat. Sader realized he had forgotten to cover the cage. Since the dog and the bird seemed to be wide awake, Sader decided to heat up the coffee and smoke a cigarette. He sat in the kitchen to do it.

He was out of a job. Old man Gibbings had canned him. The police would find the little boy, find Wanda's murderer. It was time to turn his attention to other things. Instead he found himself thinking about Tina Champlain.

The people who had known her had liked her. And yet, Sader hadn't a clear idea of the kind of woman she had been. Old man Gibbings would be hard to impress, and yet he had turned over to her unquestioningly the child his daughter had borne. She must have given an impression of honesty, decency, and kindness. Sader hadn't even seen a photograph, but he had formed a mental image. And he realized that it could be all wrong. He had learned long ago to mistrust a likeness secondhand.

Dropping aside all hearsay, one fact stood out. Mrs. Champlain had been a woman determined to be a mother.

What else was there?

She had been born a Canadian, of a very ordinary family. Where then had she met and married the brilliant young husband, the electronics engineer who had died in the crash in Colorado? What had drawn them together? Why hadn't they had children of their own?

Sader stubbed out the first cigarette, poured the coffee, sat down, lighted a second smoke and listened to the parrot cracking sunflower seeds.

Where were Mrs. Champlain's personal belongings? Surely she'd left something of herself, personal knick-knacks, pictures, legal papers. He remembered then the incinerator choked with ash, the box he had retrieved from the bottom of the trash barrel. The baby's mitten had been treasured for years, along with the locket, the ribbons, and the rest, and then it had been put out for destruction. Sader's eyes narrowed; he was remembering the bitter, frustrated aunt, Mrs. Shawell, and in memory he heard her words: *Mr. Sader, he wasn't really Tina's child. She had no right to him.* But the family had done more than disavow the child. They'd washed their hands of Tina Champlain in death. For all the interest that had been shown toward what she must have left, Tina might have been the orphan instead of her little boy.

And again, sitting in the midst of the quiet of the night, Sader had the sensation of having missed a great big chunk of the truth.

He had thought, on learning that the boy wasn't Gibbings' grandson, that the missing piece had thereby been supplied. But it hadn't followed. The part that was missing concerned Tina Champlain, her life and her motives.

Where had she found the little boy, and what had caused her to take him?

One had known the answer—Wanda Nevins. And she was dead.

The Lakeside Chapel of St. John's showed candlelight against the dull gray morning. There were a few rain spatters on the great glass panes, and when the candles flickered within the reflection moved through the raindrops like a blown breath. Sader waited outside, sizing up what was going on within. There were about a half-dozen people, and the Reverend Twining, and an infant in a long white gown. Sader decided it was a baptism.

The people came out presently and stood under the mosaic mural, and talked in a softly congratulatory, happy way among themselves, and then the men among them shook hands with Twining, and they all moved away to the cars parked at the curb. Twining nodded to Sader in recognition. "I'll be with you in a minute." He went back to the altar to extinguish the candles. Sader remained outside, smoking. He was thinking what a good-looking minister Twining was, healthy and hearty, nothing monkish or brooding about him. He wore a white lawn surplice over his suit. He had unbuttoned it, had it over his arm when he came back. He locked the chapel door and strode over to Sader. "How about a cup of coffee?"

"I'd like it. I'm doing my own cooking," Sader offered.

"Let's walk, it'll do us good."

The grass was wet. There were a lot of birds chattering in the trees beside the small lagoon. A gust of wind came up, bringing a splash of rain, and Twining glanced speculatively at the sky and said, "Well, we sure need it."

"What about praying for rain?" Sader asked. "Do much of it?"

"I'm afraid the Los Angeles Chamber of Commerce would frown on it," said Twining in dry humor. "Back where I came from—Iowa—it's not uncommon, though. When a farmer needs rain for his crops he can get pretty blunt about it to the Almighty."

They had rounded the knoll, and Twining's parsonage looked exceptionally white against the dullness of the day. Twining opened the door, let Sader precede him. Mrs. Mimms glanced at them from a door, recognized Sader. "How do you do?" She wore a starched blue dress.

"We'll have some coffee in here, please," Twining told her.

They seated themselves. Twining had dropped the surplice on a table, had taken out his pipe, filled it and didn't light it. "How are you coming along with your job?" he asked.

"I've managed to find out a few things—it would have helped to have known them from the beginning. For example, the baby Mrs. Champlain had here wasn't the one who survived her at her death."

Twining patted the tobacco in the pipe, sucked on the stem. "Two different children? How can you be sure?"

"The first child was a girl. The one she left was a boy. I guess you can't find a bigger difference than that."

"No, I guess not," Twining agreed.

"For some reason Mrs. Champlain's family refused to accept or to help the little boy. Probably Mrs. Champlain hadn't formally adopted him, or at least that's my hunch, but this business with her family goes much deeper than that. The aunt I talked to expressed hostility I couldn't account for."

Twining looked puzzled.

"The way she put it to me, was that Mrs. Champlain had no *right* to the child."

"What did she mean by it?"

"She wouldn't tell me. That's why I've come to you. Mrs. Champlain brought her aunt to one of the missionary meetings, so the aunt must not be prejudiced against your church even if she isn't a member of it."

"And you want me to talk to her?"

Sader moved his arm so that Mrs. Mimms might put down the cup of coffee on the table by him. "I didn't get anywhere with her. There's something there she wouldn't explain. It may have to do with this . . . that when Mrs. Champlain left your congregation she did more than just drop out of a church. She made a complete change, home, friends, child, everything. She became almost a different person."

Twining's expression had become somewhat blank. "What you're asking me to do is to uncover a scandal, isn't it?"

"Quite probably."

Twining began to shake his head slowly. "But you must realize, Mr. Sader, that such discovery and the passing of information to a private investigator isn't—"

"Wait a minute. Circumstances alter cases. I've never explained how this all began. It started when the grandfather of the child Mrs. Champlain first adopted came to me with an anonymous letter. The message in the letter was that the child Mrs. Champlain left was living under conditions of horrible abuse. The grandfather hired me to find him."

Twining seemed more puzzled than ever.

"I know what you're thinking. Why write to the grandfather of the first baby, the one who had died? Well, the writer seemed to have the two children confused. I suspected the old man's motives, too, when I found out the truth he hadn't told me, the change in children. But he says he feels he owes Mrs. Champlain something, and that in payment he wants to locate the little boy and make sure of his safety."

"Isn't this all a matter for the police?"

"It is, and they're working on it. But I hate to quit. I've got such a start on them," Sader explained. "Not only that, their primary interest in the case is in a murder. The girl who acted as a go-between for Mrs. Champlain's adoption of the first baby has been killed." While Twining listened with an air of fascination, Sader sketched in the facts surrounding Wanda's murder. "I don't really know whether Miss Nevins was killed in connection with the search for the boy. I just suspect it. And I want to find him."

Now Twining was leaning forward, the pipe forgotten. "Yes, I agree. This is important. If I can help . . ."

"You can talk to Mrs. Shawell."

"I'm free for the rest of the morning. I'll go at once. Just give me the address."

When Sader left a few minutes later he felt that he had made a firm ally in Twining. Perhaps the mystery of what had become of the child had intrigued the minister, or perhaps he recognized an obligation to a former member of his church, to Tina Champlain. Anyway, Sader had a hunch that Twining could get the truth out of the aunt.

When he reached the office in Long Beach, the phone was ringing. It was his attorney friend.

"Sader? News for you. There was a whopping settlement for that crash Champlain died in. He was young, a brilliant career ahead—the widow got almost a hundred thousand dollars. Plus insurance . . . there was some, I don't know just how much but I can run it down. It went to her. I don't find anything about a settlement for the child."

"What's become of the money?"

"Damned if I know. There's a will on file, disposing of about ten thousand. Left in trust for Richard Champlain, a minor."

Ricky. Sader swung the chair from the desk and dropped into it. He felt as if a closed door had suddenly opened on a totally unfamiliar room.

"Now, there is another item. A house near Laguna Beach."

"She owned a house?" Sader asked, sensing what was coming before the lawyer said it.

"She left her equity in the house to a woman named Wanda Nevins."

"Did you get the address?" Sader waited, and then the lawyer's voice scratched in his ear, the street and number, and Sader said, "The Nevins woman was living there. She was murdered there night before last."

"Oh, is that the one in the papers?"

"That's the one."

"Do you want me to check on a will—if any—left by Miss Nevins? Maybe they're bumping people off to get the house."

Something in the remark nagged, after the words were gone. "I think Miss Nevins was killed to shut her mouth. I wonder what a search of birth certificates might bring out? This Ricky Champlain. It would be about five years back."

"In an adoption, a new birth certificate is issued and all old records are sealed," the lawyer told him.

"She didn't go through the formality the second time," Sader said, thinking out loud. "I'm positive of it. Perhaps she figured a judge wouldn't legalize it since she was a widow, the kid wouldn't have a father. Or maybe there was some other reason."

"She just took the kid in?"

"I believe it." In Sader's thoughts, the sum of changes went on: a new child, a new home, a new man in Tina's life. And all old friends discarded. "She got him to take the place of a baby who had died. No, wait a minute—" Sader couldn't have said why his words rang so false. "Maybe she was just determined to be a mother. To remain a mother."

The lawyer began to check through what Sader wanted done; Sader knew that he was making notes on a scratch pad. Sader answered a few questions absent-mindedly.

"This goes on old man Gibbings' bill?"

Sader was startled for a moment. "What?"

"I'm working for Hale Gibbings, you said."

"No, send the bill to me."

"Okay."

Sader hung up, went to the outer room to retrieve the pile of mail which had been dropped in through the slot. He squatted there, sorting letters, but his mind was filled with a new idea.

Tina Champlain had defied her family to keep the little boy. There was no other logical possibility but that she had changed her way of living for the same reason. In some way it had not been possible to have Ricky and to keep the old home, the friends and church associations, her position as the widow of the young electronics expert. Therefore, it followed that Ricky was not simply a substitute for the baby that had died. He must be a child who was worth, in himself, all of the sacrifices Tina had been called upon to make.

Sader squatted there, sorting mail, letting his convictions clarify.

From the evidence it would seem that once the husband and baby girl were dead, Tina had been able to do something she'd wanted to do, all along. She had claimed something she felt was her own.

He remembered old man Perrine's remark, that Ricky had looked so much like Tina Champlain that he had found it hard to believe that Ricky wasn't her child.

However and wherever she had claimed him, Sader made a bet to himself that the trail was well covered. He had begun to guess why.

CHAPTER FOURTEEN

When Sader entered the real estate office, the little round man behind the desk bounced up and offered a hand. Sader shook it. "Thanks for seeing me right away."

"Oh, that's quite all right. Terrible thing, that young woman being killed like that. A brutal murder, according to the police. Horribly beaten, and—uh—here's a chair. I'm not sure I have anything you want to know. As I told you on the phone, I handled the sale of the house. I saw Miss Nevins a time or two downtown in Laguna, before I moved down here to Dana Point. But as for knowing either of them—"

The office was a small, portable building, painted white, set in the middle of a lot planted to ivy and blue verbena, flanked by signs extolling a group of new homes for sale. It all looked brisk and optimistic in spite of the gray sky.

"You had an office in Laguna then?"

"I handled the sale of the new homes on that side of the

hill. Had an office there, about like this one. We had fifteen homes to sell and when they were gone I worked for a short time in a downtown office, and then came here." While he talked, Mr. Evans walked to a window and adjusted the Venetian blinds to admit more light. He had an air of nervous energy, of fidgeting restlessness, in spite of the round plump frame. "They were very nice homes but the price was out of the usual range, and they moved slowly. Sold them all in the end, of course. The builder kept one for himself, top of the hill. I understand he's in Europe now."

"I'd like to know everything you remember about the sale of the house to Mrs. Champlain."

Evans returned to his chair behind the desk, sat down, gave Sader a sharp glance. "Yes. Glad to help if possible. How did you find me, by the way?"

"I checked with the County Building Department, found out who had built the house, called him—his housekeeper knew that you had sold those houses for him and where you were now. And you're right, he's in Europe."

Evans nodded. He had thin blond hair, through which his pink scalp gleamed. His fingers were round as a baby's, twiddling at the edge of the desk. "You're not a policeman?"

"I'm a private investigator. I was working on a case in which I thought Miss Nevins might have information, and now that she's dead I have to try to dig deeper, that's all."

"This was at least two years ago, that Mrs. Champlain and Miss Nevins came to look at the property." Evans hesitated, as if thinking perhaps that Sader hadn't known of the length of time. "Mrs. Champlain was older, not a lot, but she had . . . well, what you'd call a mature air, compared to Miss Nevins."

Sader remembered Wanda's smallness, the tossed black curls, the rose-petal skin and the tawny eyes, the voluptuous figure revealed by the skimpy playsuit. He made a bet with himself, Evans had spent most of the time looking at Wanda.

Evans went on, "I remember, at the time of taking them through the house, how Mrs. Champlain studied the way the place was planned and built. And how Miss Nevins raved over the big colored bathtub, and how she could decorate the bedrooms, and how much room there was for clothes in the closets. She was like a kid." He smiled, and the small twiddling fingers grew still as if they remembered some touch under them, perhaps the smoothness of Wanda's arm. "Like a kid with a new toy."

"Did Miss Nevins discuss the financial end of the matter?"

Evans thought it over, then shook his head. "No, she didn't seem to care what the place was going to cost, nor what the down payment came to. Like I said, it was Mrs. Champlain who was practical. I talked terms to her. Funny, though, when the check came in the mail it had been signed by Miss Nevins."

"But the title was vested in Mrs. Champlain?"

"That's right." Evans was frowning a little. "Now that Miss Nevins is dead, Mrs. Champlain will be moving in, I suppose."

"She's been dead about six months."

"What?" Evans seemed astonished.

"She went swimming off Catalina Island and disappeared."

"Well, now, isn't that something!" Evans sat back in his chair, forgot to twiddle his fingers. "They're both gone. Do you know who gets the house?"

"I'm not enough of a legal eagle to know that," Sader answered. "Mrs. Champlain left a little boy, a child it seems she had taken in without a formal adoption. What claim he'd have on what she left is problematical."

"She was a rich woman," Evans said with conviction.

"She gave that impression?"

"My God, she didn't blink when I told her the down payment on the house was seventeen thousand. She just nodded, as if I'd said seventeen cents."

"This is important," Sader added. "Did she give you the idea she meant to live there?"

"She sure did."

"And yet the house was never occupied by anyone but Miss Nevins."

The real estate man pursed his mouth. He replaced his fingers at the edge of the desk, appeared to wait for the beginning of a beat, then slowly and thoughtfully twiddled his hands to and fro. Sader suddenly grinned. He had realized what the little real estate man was doing.

"'Rock of Ages?'" he suggested.

Evans glanced from Sader down to his moving fingers, and after a moment of surprise, giggled. "Heh, heh.

Imaginary piano. Don't know where I ever picked up the habit. But . . . 'Nearer, My God to Thee,' wouldn't you think? Or the other one they play so much at funerals. 'End of a Perfect Day'?"

"Did Mrs. Champlain give any hint, say anything at all, to explain why she didn't move in after buying the place?"

Evans paused in the midst of a great, imaginary musical chord. "Maybe they fell out over the good-looking fellow they had along."

"There was a man with them?"

"Young. Too young for Mrs. Champlain, I'd think. But you never know. He looked like the kind who would be interested in anything if it had money with it. Hefty muscles. Deep tan. Miss Nevins called him cousin."

"Do you remember his name?"

"Don't know the name, but I remember where he lives. He rents that studio in the canyon—used to belong to that German sculptor. Eggenheim? Made religious statuary." Evans appeared to struggle with his memory.

"He made Buddhas, perhaps?"

"Eggenheim made everything. Including some with six arms. You know—India? Then he copied some of the heads at Easter Island and set them up on the hill above the studio, and one of them fell on him and crushed his legs. He lives in a sanitarium. Sold the property, the new owner rents it out. You want the address?"

"Very much."

Evans took a pencil from the desk and scribbled on the back of a business card.

Sader sat quiet, watching the plump fingers on the

pencil. The break had come so unexpectedly that he still hardly believed it. The tie-in was something he should have looked for, though. The big Buddha in Wanda's living room wasn't a souvenir of any interest in Oriental religion, but something to correspond with her décor, carted off from the disabled sculptor's studio. He should have asked about it in town, tried to trace it.

Evans flipped the card across the desk. "Take the canyon road from the beach. It's a couple of miles, the studio sits in among some trees. You'll see the stone heads on the hill when you turn off the road."

"Thanks a lot."

"I imagine the cops have already talked to this fellow, since he's a relative of Miss Nevins."

"Perhaps they have."

Evans squinted up at Sader, who had risen. "Do you suppose the cops have a clue in this murder? They've spotted the fiend already?"

Sader stood there arrested, the card in his hand. "What do you mean, fiend?"

"From the stories you hear, it had to be a fiend," Evans said firmly. "One of *them* kind." He waggled his eyebrows.

In any crime involving a girl as beautiful as Wanda, and as seductive, there was bound to be a rumor about a fiend, Sader thought. "It could be," Sader agreed. As he thanked Evans again for his information, he was thinking how lucky had been the impulse to hunt up a real estate man for information about the sale of the house. Only a man like Evans would know and remember the details of the studio's rental.

"You haven't told me what kind of case you're working on," Evans said as Sader opened the door, "but I guess with you private-eye fellows, that has to be a secret, humh?"

"I'm not working on the murder," Sader told him. "In reality we don't try it. It's police work and they wouldn't love us if we meddled. I'm looking for a missing person. A little boy. Mrs. Champlain didn't have a kid with her, by any chance?"

Evans shook his head. "Nary a sign. I wouldn't have taken her for a mother, that's for sure."

"What do you mean by that?"

Evans gazed at him blankly. "Damned if I know. I guess I just expect a woman with kids—with even one kid—to have a stocking seam out of kelter. Or a petticoat hem showing."

Into Sader's memory popped the thing Mrs. Bowen had told him, that the aunt had seemed something of a hick; and he should have caught it then, he realized. *In contrast to her niece*, Mrs. Shawell was a hick. It had to be.

"Mrs. Champlain was dressed pretty well, is that it?"

"By golly, I've seen 'em all in my business," Evans declared, "and she was the slickest thing in a long spell."

"But not better than Miss Nevins?"

"Miss Nevins was . . . well, I'd call her kind of cuddly," Evans said with a hint of sly camaraderie. "You know, soft and cute, little black curls and dimples. Mrs. Champlain looked like those models you see in the fashion ads."

It wasn't a thing anyone else had told him; but he knew that he hadn't been asking about Tina Champlain, but about Gibbings' daughter, and somehow he'd gotten the two confused. The things he'd learned about Kit Gibbings, the dowdy sense of style, the feeling of a loving and obedient and patient nature, he'd somehow transferred to the other woman. The more fool he, he thought. "What part did the man play in the buying of the house?"

"Not a damned word."

"Well, thanks a lot for all you've told me."

"Ah, it wasn't anything."

The last Sader saw of the real estate man, Evans was sitting with fingers poised, ready to strike an opening chord on the rim of the desk. Sader got into his car and headed north again. In downtown Laguna Beach he turned right into the canyon highway. The sea wind followed, funneling through the narrow cleft in the coastal hills. He heard it whistle against the window. In about two miles he found a six-foot redwood fence, much weathered, the name EGGENHEIM painted on a board above a mailbox. He parked the car and went to the gate, which sagged ajar. Inside was a wilderness of eucalyptus and shaggy palms. Half-hidden on the side of the hill above was what looked like a red barn. Sader went in, climbing the pathway among the trees. It was very quiet. The gray light made it all look kind of sleepy. There wasn't even a bird chirping.

The pathway circled the red building. On its north side a great expanse of glass tilted to the sky. Sader listened at the door, heard nothing. He opened it and looked in. The interior was a great barren room with a lot of unfinished sculpture and a smell of clay. At the far end Sader could see the stairs to a loft. He shut the door and looked around him. The pathway went on, winding among the trees toward the top of the hill. Sader climbed it.

He came out below a bald knob where dead grasses quivered under the touch of breeze. Here and there, grotesque and enormous, were the heads the sculptor had erected; they faced toward the invisible Pacific. Not of stone; Sader saw that the tip of the nose was broken on one, that another had a great crack through the center of the forehead, in both cases exposing a framework of wire and lathe. Apparently Eggenheim had made them by erecting a frame and plastering it over with concrete—not as solid as the originals on Easter Island but still nothing you'd want to fall over on you, Sader thought.

None of them—there were six in all—stood quite erect. Probably the effect of ages of settling into the earth was deliberate, Sader decided; but one was cocked at a sharper angle than the rest and he thought it might be the one that had crippled its creator, pushed half-erect after the accident. At any rate, Eggenheim couldn't have asked for a more impressive nor a weirder monument. They were fantastic.

Sader climbed on to the top of the knoll, where he could see the surrounding country. Invisible from the path he had climbed was a smaller building, also painted red, hidden among the trees on a far spur of the hill. A fainter path led down toward it.

He started down, and then something warned him—a prickling sense of walking into the unknown. He couldn't name the feeling. It was as old as time, older than the originals of the great stone heads above him on the knoll. He missed a step, though he didn't pause. He kept his eyes on the windows. They were curtained; he couldn't see through them. The path ended in a small flat graveled terrace. Sader put out a hand to knock.

The door came open before he reached it. Brent Perrine looked at him and said, "What the hell are you doing here?" Then he caught Sader by the front of his coat and drew back his fist and slammed it at Sader's head. Sader had only a moment to jerk aside.

In the instant of ducking Sader glimpsed the big room beyond, the signs of search in it. The wind from Brent's fist fanned his cheek. He brought up his clenched hands sharply to break Brent's hold on his clothes, at the same time dropping right. Brent didn't let go, and there was the sound of tearing cloth. Sader put a quick uppercut where it would do the most good. Brent was big and solid, but not fast in a fight. Perhaps he'd been using his old man for a sparring partner too long. He yanked his head back and shook it. Then he dragged Sader into the room.

Sader warded off another punch, felt his left arm go numb under it. He looked around. To his right was a spindly legged table, very ornate, very much not the kind of thing you'd expect in a woodland studio, and on it was a small Persian coffee jug of worked brass. Sader picked up the little jug in his right fist and aimed it at Brent; the rim of the heavy base caught Brent over the eye and laid the skin open. Blood spurted. Brent let out a yell of fury.

He was heavy, as solid as hell under Sader's light pummeling. Sader had had judo training years ago during the war, and he tried to get a hold on Brent, but now Brent had him pinned against the wall. The table had fallen and Brent had crushed it with splintery crackings.

Sader tried to get the copper jug into position again, but Brent chopped at his wrist, and the jug went flying. The next blow hit Sader on the cheekbone and he had the eerie sensation of hearing his own skull creak, the teeth moving against his tongue, followed by a quick salty flavor of blood. For the first time Sader got the feeling he was going to come out second best. He kept the numb left arm up, protecting his chin, but Brent was close and fought like a cat, close-in, wearing him down.

God, I'm getting old, Sader thought. He felt the fifty years sweep down on him, beating with blue lights behind his eyes, tearing the breath out of his lungs. He punched Brent on the collar bone, a blow no heftier than a fly's.

"By God, I'm plenty damned sick of you!" Brent grunted, and grabbed Sader's head between his hands and shoved it hard against the wall, then yanked forward to slam back again. For Sader stars burst against the darkening room. He tried to knee the younger man, to jerk free again, and Brent kicked him, numbing an ankle. Then Brent picked him up bodily and threw him into a chair. It must have been something like the table, small and spindly, because he went down into it as if into a nest of collapsing straw. There was the smell of broken wood and he felt the prick of splinters through his clothes, into his flesh.

He tried to extricate himself quickly, get to his feet.

Brent came to him, stood there, took careful aim with his boot, smashed it toe-first into Sader's face. A red glare burst in Sader's right temple, flooding his sight. He crawled forward, groping, and Brent kicked again. There was a shock, starting near his left shoulder, that ran like a live electric wire, threading bone to bone, all the way down the numb arm to the fingertips, and jumping down his body from rib to rib.

"I'll teach you." The words rolled through an enormous silence, while Sader lay on his face, clutching what was left of consciousness.

There were three more kicks, three jars that shook him without pain, as if he stood somewhere outside his fallen body, immune to feeling. He lay in darkness, listening. He heard Brent walk around the room, he heard the rustle of paper and cloth, the clink of glassware, and he knew down there in the dim quiet that Brent was hunting for something.

When enough of the haze had cleared away, when he could control the numbed body, Sader staggered to his feet. The fight must go on.

It must go on because somewhere a kid waited, needing help, and in Sader's rocked mind one thing was clear: *it was up to him to find him.*

CHAPTER FIFTEEN

He looked around, squinting against the aching red haze, but Brent wasn't in the room. Sader listened, heard the scrape of drawers on their runners, the growling monotone with which Brent greeted whatever he was looking at. Sader staggered clear of the wreck of the chair and the broken table. He went to a window, leaned there to suck in air. His ribs hurt. His left arm hung useless. One side of his head beat with a pulse like a roaring surf. No shaking dislodged it.

He turned again to examine the room. Drawers hung open in all the cabinets, their contents littered the carpet, but still the picture was plain. Someone had traveled far and brought home treasures to furnish this place. There were ivory figurines and jade elephants, inlaid tables, lamps of worked brass like the little coffee jug, and the carpet was blue and silver, an old chaste pattern of Persian yarns. There were teakwood chests, plus a lot of the gilded and fragile kind of stuff that went with the table and chair that was broken.

It had been brought from far away and put here, hidden away in this house in the grove, and Sader wondered if it belonged to the sculptor and if he had left it here for the tenant, or whether Wanda's cousin could own it.

Brent came to the doorway. His hands were empty. He looked tired. The wound over his eye had bled down his cheek. His eye was puffed. He said, "I thought you'd be gone by now, you damned meddler."

"Just tell me where the boy is and I'll leave you alone."

Brent shook his head. "I don't know where he is."

"Is that what you're doing here—looking for some clue to his whereabouts?"

"It's none of your damned business what I'm doing." Still, Sader thought, Brent looked a little uneasy, as if Sader had skirted the truth.

"If you don't kill that old man of yours," Sader said, "he's going to kill you. Not that it would be a great loss in either case. But you and him know a lot you're not telling. Probably you borrowed a lot of money from Tina Champlain and then drowned her to keep from repaying the loan. But who could prove it? Wise up, why don't you? I just want the kid."

Brent's angry eyes moved across the windows, the view of the trees. In spite of the way the scrap had turned out, he had a puzzled, almost defeated look. "Do you really just want the boy?"

"That's what I keep trying to tell you."

"How much will you pay for him?"

Into Sader's mind flashed the figures of his bank balance, a little more than two hundred dollars. Two hundred and sixty-three, something like that. He knew what he could depend on from his partner Scarborough. About the same. "Five thousand. Maybe ten. It would depend on how soon we got the information."

Brent's expression, as far as Sader could judge, was almost indifferent. He's covering up, Sader thought, he doesn't really know where Ricky is, he's just talking to cover up whatever he came here to do, or he's trying to think of some new place to look for whatever is supposed to be hidden here. He said, "Well, they might go as high as twenty thousand. I'd have to check first."

"Twenty thousand." Brent seemed to consider it, weighing it against some other values, perhaps the resources of whoever had Ricky. "When would you know for sure?"

Sader thought, What's he up to? He's pulling my leg, his mind's on something else entirely. "We'd have to have some guarantee from you, some proof you know what you're talking about. Look, you must have had to share Tina's money with your old man, to keep his mouth shut. This would be yours, *all* yours."

Brent's look, for an unguarded moment, was that of a man who hears a dangerous truth spoken aloud. They *had* gotten money out of Tina, then. The old man had claimed his share.

Sader said, "You must want like hell to clear out and get away from your old man. He's a mess, a drunk, and he's dangerous. He takes pot shots at you when you have an argument, and then you have to beat him up. I guess when he's pretty drunk he threatens to tell somebody about what really happened to Tina Champlain."

The shape of Brent's cheeks flattened, his shoulders moved, and Sader knew he had goaded him about as much as he would take.

"So this twenty thousand—even if it doesn't look like much after what you got from Tina—this will still get you away from him and let you have a boatyard of sorts, all your own."

"You're full of bull," Brent said, but he wasn't worked up about it. He was thinking again of whatever it was he had looked for here, and hadn't found. "I'll tell you what, though. About that money. Why don't you come to my place in Wilmington and bring the cash? Later. Say around ten o'clock?"

"I can try."

"That's fine."

Sader knew in that moment that Brent had other plans entirely.

"You'd better get out of here now, and don't come back."

Sader went to the door. His left arm had begun to tingle and he could move his fingers. He went out into the afternoon sunlight, the glare burning hot under his eyelids, and he had a moment of sick staggering. Then he got his bearings. He climbed the knoll to the big stone heads that looked toward the far-off sea. When he got to the shadow of the first one, he sat down on the ground and shut his eyes. The earth whirled.

He had to think, to figure this out. There was still a job to do. Not for money. Hell, no. He was above money. He was brave and noble, a private eye out of a TV series, doing it all for the love of it. He wasn't working for old man Gibbings, who was a crud except for that out-landish streak of decency that made him want to find a starving kid. He wasn't working for Mr. Gibbings' no-longer-virgin daughter, because, hell, she didn't even know a man named Sader existed. He wasn't working for Ricky, because Ricky was a mirage. He was doing it . . . yes, dammit . . . because he was like a frog in a rut and there was only one way to hop. Sader wanted to laugh at this, but his head hurt.

He thought back to that moment of instant attack, when he had met Brent at the door, and a new idea came to him. Brent had been on edge, ready to jump anybody who came in, ready to defend himself with his fists. He had been expecting somebody all right, but it couldn't have been Sader. Sader hadn't known, until a brief time before, that the canyon place even existed. So Brent was nervous and jumpy because of somebody else, the real tenant of the place, Wanda's cousin, the crewcut juvenile who had taken Ricky from Mrs. Cecil's house.

Whatever Brent had been looking for must be some-thing worth the trouble if Crewcut came in and caught him. The only thing Brent had seemed interested in up to now was owning his own boatyard, which took money. Maybe more money than he'd already gotten out of Tina. Was there money here? Sader stared through the glaring light at the grove and the half-hidden house. He got to his feet, leaning against the concrete, the backside of the big stone head, with clumps of broken cement in the dirt at its base. He looked at the red house and worked his left arm, feeling life seep back into it, the fingers stinging and the wrist afire with pain. Then he heard the slam of a door. Brent would be coming along.

He ran hurrying down the opposite side of the knoll to the gate, went out to his car, got into it and headed down the canyon road. At the intersection in Laguna Beach, he pulled in behind a service station and waited. Pretty soon Brent came down the canyon drive in an Olds sedan, black with a cream top, and headed north. Sader followed, fighting traffic to keep within sight of the other car. Brent kept up a pretty good clip but still he wasn't exactly rushing to get there, and Sader got the idea he might be mulling things over, making plans as he drove.

When they swept through Long Beach on Route 101 and headed for Wilmington, Sader knew where Brent was going. Now he wanted to get ahead of Brent, beat him to the house, but there didn't seem to be a chance. He didn't know of any short cuts. He was trying to figure out what he could do, when Brent suddenly pulled the Olds in to the curb in front of a liquor store. Sader roared by in a burst of traffic.

He parked in the block behind the Perrine place and ran across the weedy lots to the back door. He knocked, waited. He thought he heard a grunt from upstairs, then a snore. He opened the kitchen door and went in, walked to the hall, listened again, then went softly up the stairs.

There were no further sounds, except that the old house creaked a little. Sader went to the open door of the old man's room. Unexpectedly there was the odor of fresh linen.

Someone had put clean sheets on the old man's bed, a case on the pillow, and there was a clean blanket folded at the foot. Ralph Perrine lay in the bed, in an atmosphere of almost hospital-like cleanness. Sader stepped close. Ralph Perrine was asleep. There were patches of adhesive bandages on the worst of the bruises. He breathed with a hoarse dragging sound, as if he had run a long way and had fallen down to die.

Curiously, Sader put a hand down to touch the bare shoulder, but Ralph Perrine didn't stir. Sader turned quickly to the hall. From outside and below was the sound of a car's motor. He looked around and found a tiny room off the hall, which must have been built originally for a sewing closet; there were shelves at the back and an ironing board flapped up against the wall, and a long-ago smell of starch and cotton.

He kept a quarter-inch crack to see through.

Brent came up the stairs. Sader stepped back so quickly that he forgot to ease his weight, and a board creaked and for a minute he thought Brent would notice. But Brent had eyes only for the door of his father's room.

Sader could hear him walking around in there, then a sudden sharp order for the old man to wake up. "I've brought you a bottle of muscatel. Sit up and have some. I want to talk to you, and I want you to understand what I'm saying."

Sader couldn't hear any reply from Ralph Perrine. There were slapping sounds then that made Sader flinch.

"You damned dirty old wino! I hope you're dying. I don't give a damn any more."

There was a gurgling reply that died into mumbles.

"I could have married her if it hadn't been for you. A nice girl. And then it was too late. She'd gone overboard."

There were more slaps, then a scuffling noise as if the old man was trying to get away. Then he cried distinctly, "Brent! Brent, don't!"

"You're going to have a bath and get some clean clothes on. Then we're going to take a trip. We'll go down to Ensenada, go down the coast into Mexico, and we'll fish, we'll take some time out."

After a moment they came out, Brent almost carrying the old man, and went down the hall to the bathroom. Sader could hear water running, could hear the old man's querulous mumbling. There was a sudden splash and a loud gasping yelp, and Brent said bitterly, "I ought to let you drown."

He left the old man in the tub and went back to the room, and Sader heard dresser drawers being opened and shut. When he went back into the bath, the old man whined, "Don't always blame me because she went overboard. It didn't have nothing to do with us."

"You wouldn't keep your damned mouth shut," Brent said, almost yelling. "You had to keep talking and talking, you couldn't let it alone, how the kid looked like her. And then pretty soon she couldn't take any more. And you did it!"

"Look, we're covered. How can that detective find anything?"

"Dry yourself. Here's a towel."

"Is he giving you trouble? Hell, he's fifty and you've got it on him by twenty pounds. I learned you to fight."

"The only one I'd really like to beat up is you," Brent said savagely.

They came back down the hall, Brent guiding his father, who was buttoning the cuffs on a clean shirt. At the bedroom door the old man said, "I want a drink!"

"I said I'd bought you a bottle."

"That cold water shocked hell out of me."

"It wasn't cold."

Ralph Perrine sat down on the edge of his bed, rubbed the wet hair out of his eyes. "You got some money? You made a touch somewhere?"

"I've got what I walked out of here with this morning."

Ralph Perrine was lifting the wine bottle to his lips. Brent turned away as if unwilling to look. "I'm going to pack some clothes." He went out, leaving his father sitting there on the edge of the bed.

Ralph Perrine looked cautiously at the doorway, then tilted the wine bottle—Sader had never seen such continuous swallowing. When he had finished drinking, he fell over on his side.

From Brent's room came the snap of a suitcase lock. Brent came into the hall carrying a brown bag, with a jacket over his arm. He stood for a long moment looking in at his father. Then he set the case down on the floor and went in to stand beside the bed. Sader saw him reach down, lift the bottle and stare at the level of its contents.

"I used to give a damn," Brent said, as if in surprise at himself. "I used to worry about what might happen to you and I guess that's why I was going to take you with me now."

He stood for a moment waiting, and from the bed came a heavy snore. Brent suddenly tossed the bottle of wine onto the clean sheet. "It was a crazy idea. You'd find some way to ruin things, get us both in dutch." He turned and went out, picked up the case, and ran downstairs. In another moment Sader heard the car start.

When the car had backed, when the sound of the motor was gone, Sader went downstairs and located the phone, called Jackson's office. "One of your suspects is headed for Mexico. Brent Perrine." As he stood there in the musty living room, waiting to fill Jackson in on it, he wondered where Brent had parked his car when he had gone to the canyon house in Laguna. It must have been out of sight inside some shrubbery, Sader decided. "Yes, I ran into him earlier today," Sader told Jackson. "I guess you know that Wanda Nevins had a cousin in Laguna. He answers the description of the man who took Tina Champlain's little boy away after she died. I think it all ties in somewhere, that Brent knows what's happened to the child. He might even have killed the girl. He's money hungry, and she had some."

Jackson's replies were guarded, so Sader figured he wasn't alone, he was with somebody and didn't want them to know he was sharing information with a private dick.

"I ran into Perrine. He was searching the house where Wanda's cousin lives. No one else was there." Sader shifted the phone from his left hand; the arm ached.

"We haven't been able to locate the man who is Wanda Nevins' relative," Jackson said carefully. "If you have a description, we need it."

"He's young, tanned, athletic in build. Drives a convertible and dresses pretty sharp. He was with Wanda Nevins and Mrs. Champlain when they bought the house at

Laguna. The real estate agent thinks he was pretty good friends with Tina Champlain."

"What do you mean? Some kind of gigolo?"

"Could be. He's got some fancy furniture in his house. It cost money. Somebody's."

Through the windows of the darkening room, Sader could see the twilight sky above the Palos Verdes hills. There was a sudden taste of exhaustion, as sharp as that of blood, in his mouth, and he was aware that he had taken a beating, that he hadn't had any dinner, that he was so tired that he could have dropped where he stood to sleep.

The phone trembled in his grip. He felt that he was alone in a room full of ghosts.

CHAPTER SIXTEEN

When he had finished talking to Jackson, Sader went back upstairs. Ralph Perrine had turned over on his back, got his feet up on the sheets, and was snoring. Sader went across to Brent's room. Even though Brent had packed hastily here a few moments ago, the room was still in order. Sader inspected the closet, where several suits hung, then looked through the dresser drawers. The impression he got was that not only was Brent a tidy, cleanly person but that he took care to keep little on hand concerning his personal life. There were very few personal souvenirs among his belongings.

In what was there, Sader found a snapshot that he kept. It showed Brent and a small boy on the deck of a cabin cruiser. The boat was tied up at a dock somewhere–Sader thought that the background looked like Balboa–and in the near distance a woman in a bathing suit seemed just to have turned from the camera.

There was no date, no notation of any kind on the back of the picture, and Sader had no way of being sure, but his hunch told him this was Tina's little boy. Perhaps the woman in the background was Tina herself. He wished that she'd been facing the camera.

He went downstairs and let himself out, closed the house and walked to his car. By now the Highway Patrol would have an eye out for Brent. Probably they'd collar him at the border, where explanations would be more obviously in order.

Sader felt too rumpled, too grimy, and too bruised to face a crowd in a restaurant. He drove to a small neighborhood market and picked up some hamburger, some bread and butter, cheese and tomatoes, and went on out to Scarborough's place in Los Alamitos. As he drove, he tormented himself with the memory of his neglect about calling the Reverend Twining. There might be news for him there.

At the house the lonesome dog greeted him with jumps and barks, and the parrot raised hell in his cage because sometime during the day he had emptied his water cup and nobody had been here to refill it. Sader fed and watered the pair of them, then tried to call Twining, but found the number busy. He went up and drew a tub of warm water and soaked himself. He inspected his left arm; a couple of tendons hurt like hell when he clenched his hand, and there were dark bruises above the wrist. I was lucky at that, Sader thought, I'm so damned out of condition and he was so cute. When he had toweled and put on a robe he went to the bathroom mirror and sized up his face. There was a puffed mark where Brent had caught him on the cheek. It wasn't too bad.

He went downstairs and fried the hamburger with

onions, heated the buttered bread in the oven, sliced toma-toes. When he had eaten he began to feel sleepy.

He went into the front room and sat down to smoke. Then he remembered the snapshot and went upstairs, got it out of his coat pocket, took it back down with him. He turned on a lamp and studied the picture.

The age of the boy would be about right, five or so. He wasn't big for his age, but there was a past-five maturity about him. He had dark eyes, dark hair, and even though Brent was tanned from exposure, the kid's natural coloring was almost as dark. Remembering what old man Perrine had said, that Mrs. Champlain and the child resembled each other, Sader bent close to study the features. But the boy seemed, in the picture, to be a very ordinary-looking kid. If he resembled anyone, Sader thought, it was ten thousand other kids his age. Something hung from his neck on a string . . . a religious medal, perhaps. He was sitting hunched inside the curve of Brent's arm, hugging his knees. On Brent's features was a look of complete indif-ference. The child's look was guarded.

He was a scared kid, Sader thought, even then.

Who had taken the snapshot? Brent's old man? It could have been some passer-by who had obliged with the cam-era, or Tina herself, providing the woman in the snapshot hadn't been Tina after all.

The phone rang. Sader laid the snapshot on the table beneath the lamp, and answered. It was the Reverend Twining.

"Mr. Sader? I've been trying to get you at your office. Your answering service gave me this number."

"Sorry. I should have thought to leave it with you."

"Yes. Well, I wondered if you could come up for a talk tonight. I have something I want to discuss. Not good news, I'm afraid, and not anything I can discuss over the phone."

"Do you know where the boy is?"

"No. This concerns Mrs. Champlain's motive for taking him."

The parrot made a rustling commotion in his cage, and Sader jumped. "I'll be up as soon as I can get there. It'll take a little time to drive it."

"Well, I rarely get to bed before midnight anyway," said Twining. "I'll have the coffee hot."

"Thanks. I'll see you."

Twining had done him a favor, had done part of the job for him, and had had to run him down to tell him about it. Sader felt grim. He went up and dressed again. The dog followed him to the door, disappointed, and the parrot squawked in his cage, the tone implying that Sader was a sad failure as a zookeeper.

Driving up the freeway, Sader occupied himself with thoughts of Brent Perrine. Brent hadn't reacted to the offer of money as Sader had been convinced he would. He hadn't gone home and checked to make sure the old man was staying put, and then taken off to wherever the kid was hidden. He had gone to get his dad and to clear out.

He had wanted the money. That fact had gleamed in his eyes. But something had blocked him.

Was he Wanda's murderer? Was there something about revealing where the kid was that would reveal him as the killer, too?

186

Wanda had died brutally, and Brent was a big strong man, well able to beat a woman to death as Wanda had been beaten. It was true that he seemed to have brief spells of compassion, such as he'd shown his father; but these could simply be the split half of a schizophrenic personality.

Twining met him at the door. The place looked quiet and peaceful. Sader had driven past the little chapel, and through the glass walls had seen an altar light gleaming. He thought that the young minister looked tired, sort of worried, too. Twining took him into the parlor and offered a chair, brought a hot cup of coffee from another room and put it on the table by Sader.

"I went to see Mrs. Champlain's aunt. I had to wait—she was out on an errand—and then when I got back here other things kept me busy. I'm sorry it's been this long before I got hold of you."

"My fault, too, I should have checked earlier than I did. I called in once, during the afternoon." Sader waited, wanting Twining to get down to whatever he had to tell.

Twining was in his chair, the unlighted pipe in his fingers. "Mrs. Shawell was at first very secretive. I had quite a time convincing her I wasn't a private detective in minister's garb. Apparently you gave her a fright. You see, the thing she's guarding is her dead niece's reputation. Did she insist to you—as she did to me—that the child couldn't actually belong to Mrs. Champlain?"

"Well, she insisted that Tina Champlain had no right to him."

"I kept talking on that point to her, since it seemed moot. I said that the only reason Mrs. Champlain would have taken the little boy was because she loved him and must have thought he needed her. And then Mrs. Shawell began to cry, and said no, that wasn't it at all. She told me that Mrs. Champlain's motive had been something else entirely." Suddenly Twining leaned back in the chair, looked dejectedly into the pipe bowl, and shook his head. "I don't want to be a party to any feast of gossip."

"I know how to keep my mouth shut. And I've got to find the kid," Sader said doggedly.

"Yes. Well, perhaps this will throw some light. You know that Mr. Champlain was an electronics engineer, a very good man in his field. He was constantly traveling, most of the time by air. He went all over the world."

"I had surmised as much."

"Naturally while he was traveling Mrs Champlain was left alone. They had a mountain cabin at one time, up in the Tehachapi district, and sometimes she'd go there by herself, though her aunt worried about it when she did. Then once, just after she'd spent some time in the mountains and just as her husband returned from a month or so abroad, Mrs. Champlain had an hysterical breakdown and had to be sent to the hospital."

"The aunt thinks that something happened in the mountains?"

"She told me that Tina Champlain underwent a change from which she never recovered. There were long months during which Mrs. Champlain didn't come around. Letters went unanswered. Once someone called from Tina's church, asked how she was . . . it seemed she was supposed to be in some sanitarium."

"I can guess what's in Mrs. Shawell's mind," Sader said. "She thinks that Tina Champlain may have been attacked, raped in that lonely cabin, and later bore a child—the little boy she took in after her husband and the first child were dead."

Twining nodded.

"I can't understand Mrs. Shawell turning against the kid the way she did—not even checking up after Tina's death to make sure he had proper care or even enough to eat. Not offering him a home."

"They're a Canadian family of old French descent and have lived for generations in a little town in eastern Canada. I'm not offering this as an excuse. But I can understand Mrs. Shawell's rejection, particularly when she added that her niece had been a rather wild young girl and had been expected to come a cropper by disapproving neighbors."

Sader was frowning. "What did she say about the adoption of the little girl?"

Twining shrugged. "Very little. She said Mrs. Champlain loved the little girl and did everything possible to keep her alive. You know, since Champlain died in a plane crash there may have been a lot of insurance, even a settlement with the company."

"There was."

"The medical care of the baby girl may have accounted for quite a bit of it."

"I agree, and I'm surprised I hadn't thought of it." Sader

was actually sore at himself for the oversight. Chunks of Tina's inheritance seemed to have vanished down a rathole—he had suspected Wanda Nevins and the Perrines of accounting for most of it—and all the time it could have been paid out in hospital and doctor's bills, in an effort to save the baby who had been born with a defective heart.

Wryly, he thought, in passing, of Gibbings and Gibbings' money. The old man had saved himself some hefty expense, getting rid of the baby as quickly as he had.

Twining went on, "The aunt told me all of this . . . hinted at most of it, actually, after I had convinced her that I was a real minister and that she could trust me. I feel that I am betraying a confidence, and yet . . ." He suddenly took out matches and lighted the tobacco and puffed with an air of anger. ". . . I want the child found, too, Mr. Sader. There's a spot in the New Testament—maybe you're not much of a Bible reader—"

"I guess I know that one," Sader said. "Something about *as you do to the least of these*, isn't it?"

"It occurred to me, then, that if Mrs. Champlain knew where her real child was, knew how to go about reclaiming him, she had kept contact with people we know nothing about."

"Well, that's pretty obvious."

"So—how do you find them?"

Sader thought about it; not for the first time. "The only way I can work is through the people I've already met, the ones I've talked to who knew Tina Champlain while she was alive. There must be a lead there. I just haven't seen it. Somewhere the two parts of her life coincided. Some-where the life she led here, while she went to your church and knew the people in it, and lived as Champlain's loving wife, overlaps that other existence down in Santa Monica. I just haven't dug deep enough."

Twining regarded him thoughtfully. "This girl who was murdered—wasn't she a sort of carry-over into Mrs. Champlain's new life?"

"Yes. And so was a man I can't locate, a husky cousin of hers. They seem to have known Mrs. Champlain right up to the end. In fact, I have an idea that Wanda Nevins knew more about Mrs. Champlain's affairs than anyone else, that she not only arranged the adoption of the baby girl, but found the boy for Mrs. Champlain when she wanted him."

"Have you talked to the police, on the chance Miss Nevins left some clue?"

"They haven't found the little boy. If they had, I'd know it." Sader got up restlessly and walked around, matching his steps to the pattern of the rug. "There's another person I want to talk to. I'll need your help. I want to contact Dr. Bell, the minister who was here while Mrs. Champlain was a member of your church."

"He's teaching now."

"Yes, I know that. And probably he wouldn't answer questions over the phone unless I had you to vouch for me."

Twining glanced at the mantel clock. "It's late now. I'd hate to disturb him. Suppose we put through a call in the morning?"

"I guess that will do."

Twining seemed curious. "Do you expect him to know the truth about what happened in the mountain cabin?"

"If anything did happen. While she lived out here, Mrs. Champlain seems to have tried to be a good church member. Probably she began to break away at about the time the aunt said she began to avoid her—but still, she may have talked to Dr. Bell, may have asked his help. He would have done what he could. If we can just convince him that he won't be violating a confidence, he can help us."

"We'll give it a try. I'm going to keep working with you until that little boy is found," Twining said firmly.

"Thanks for what you've done already."

Twining got to his feet and held out his hand, shook Sader's. "Well, we have an inkling as to her motive for wanting the little boy. He must have been her own, after all. But we haven't an inkling who kept him during the years she had the other baby—or who has him now."

"Maybe it's right under our noses," Sader said, "and we just can't see it."

Driving past the chapel a few minutes later, Sader studied it in the glow of altar light. It wasn't a big place; Twining's congregation couldn't be over a couple of hundred or so. It looked like a sparkling phantom, sugar-frosted, there among the trees. All at once Sader remembered that he had not been in or even near a church for years, and he felt a sudden curiosity about Twining, what the young minister would say in the pulpit, and he made a halfhearted promise to come up some Sunday and listen.

He drove to the freeway, went straight through the heart of L.A. and on down to the beach. He turned south there. It was late, there wasn't a lot of traffic. He hit Huntington Beach at midnight, on the dot, and a few minutes later he'd left Newport behind. When he reached the outskirts of Laguna Beach he turned in at the road that led up to Wanda's house. The place was dark, locked, and there was a Sheriff's seal on the door. Sader got back into the car, drove on into town, turned left up the canyon road. He had made up his mind that the middle of the night might be a good time to see who or what was in the sculptor's studio.

There were no cars parked at the gate. He went up the hill through the trees, and the red barn seemed to sit there in a listening stillness. The panes of its north light gleamed under the glow from the sky. On the knoll the great stone heads had a look of peaceful and mysterious dignity. They looked seaward through the night. They were at the same time, more remote and yet more real than by day.

He passed them with the familiar sense that their gaze followed, his steps echoing, and then below in the other house he saw a light. He walked more slowly, trying to be silent.

Through the uncurtained window the room seemed much as he had seen it earlier. There were still signs of Brent's searching, but the broken stuff had been cleared away. But what sat in the middle of the floor was nothing Sader could have hoped to find here.

A small boy.

And a dog.

The boy wore faded pajamas and he sat hunched as he had in the snapshot with Brent, his eyes fixed on the door, hugging his knees. The likeness was unmistakable.

The dog was a copy of the brute Wanda had brought to his office. The dog had been asleep beside the boy, but now having heard Sader's approach, had lifted his head and tuned his ears.

CHAPTER SEVENTEEN

Without leaving the window, Sader stretched and touched the doorknob, rattled it gently. In a moment the dog was on his feet, neck elongated, lips drawn back to bare the big teeth. He was a ripping-machine, something created to destroy the enemy. Well, I know what he's here for, Sader thought; he's here to keep everyone away from the kid. With his nails, Sader tapped on the wall beside the door, showing his face through the pane. He called, "Hey, Ricky, come let me in!"

There was a chance someone else was in there, of course, but something about the setup, the kid alone in the middle of the floor as if he'd been put there, the dog guarding, said not, and Sader took the chance.

The boy moved his gaze slowly and unwillingly from the door over to stare at Sader, and then he suddenly bent his head and covered his eyes with his hands. Sader thought he looked awfully little, awfully alone too, hunched like that. The lamp behind him cast his shadow, and it wasn't very big either. The dog's shadow looked like a horse's.

"I'm a friend. I just want to talk to you, I just want to make sure you're all right."

Without removing his hands from his eyes, Ricky shook his head. This, too, followed some previous command, Sader sensed. "Aw, you can walk over to the window here and let me look at you. He won't care about that," Sader wheedled, wondering himself whether by *he* he meant the brute or the man who had left his instructions.

The boy peeped at him through his fingers. Then he took his hands away from his eyes, got to his feet, and tried to get to the window. The dog was no fool; he kept getting in the way. He showed his teeth at Ricky but Ricky wasn't dismayed, he pulled and tugged at the big ears, turning the head, so that the dog moved on behind him. Ricky got about five feet from the window and stopped, regarding Sader with suspicion, and suddenly Sader was struck with a new uncertainty: What the hell he was doing here? He'd been so sure the kid had to be rescued, but here he was, no obvious bruises or contusions, no broken arms or legs, no eagerness for help, no tears.

Then Sader took a second look and saw the hollow eyes, the fragile line of the skull showing through the flesh, betraying starvation. Something rose in his throat and he almost vomited.

"Turn around."

"Who are you?" Ricky asked through the pane.

"Just turn around, Ricky."

Turn around and lift the tops of your pajamas, and then pull down the seat, so I can look for marks of beating. . . .

Otherwise, they can say you've just been sick–

196

"Turn around, won't you?"

"I can't."

"What do you mean, you can't?" The sudden breeze touched the sweat on Sader's face; he hadn't known it was there.

"Because I'm supposed to stay in the middle of the rug. And I'm not supposed to talk to anybody."

"Who brought you here?"

"My m . . . The lady."

"Isn't there a man living here?"

Ricky nodded. "Yes, there's Jeffry. He's big."

"He and the lady are partners?"

"I thought he was my father. I mean, once I did." Ricky's hollow eyes blinked, then filled with tears; blinked again and the tears were gone.

"When he took you away from Mrs. Cecil?"

Ricky shivered inside the baggy pajamas. "Yes."

"What does Jeffry call this lady? The one who keeps you now?"

"He calls her Mrs. Lasriss."

Sader wanted to shake his head, as if something were clinging to it, something that scuttled and nibbled at the edge of memory, something . . . yes, dammit, something to do with Twining! A sheer sticky thread across the edge of his mind like a thread of spider's web across the face, something you had to pluck off in horror!

"Do you like her?"

"She whips me." He said it simply, looking at Sader through the pane, and Sader knew then that all the reasons for whipping, for starving, had been explained to

Ricky and that once he got Ricky outside that door he would know them too.

"How about coming away with me?" Sader blurted, though he should have known better. Ricky stepped back two feet and looked for a place to sit, and Sader knew—with a pang—that the child had learned this response: to sit and fold arms and endure while hell went on. "Goddamit—" Then Sader got control and remembered a few things, and said, "Hey, do you like ice cream, Ricky?"

Ricky was sitting down now. He was ready to fold his arms and hide his eyes, because there were things you couldn't endure otherwise and this might turn out to be one of them. "Yes," he said, muffled.

"Well, I'll buy ice cream if you can get out without the dog getting out too."

"I don't know how."

"Will you come to the door and try to help me?"

Ricky was still suspicious. "Doing what?"

"Holding the dog."

"You can't hold him," Ricky explained in a sober, adult manner. "He bites after a while. You can touch him a little, you can even pull and guide him where you want him to go. But if he sees something bad and you try to hold him back from it, you'll be torn to pieces."

Someone had explained the mechanics of Bruce—if it was Bruce—to Ricky, so there wouldn't be any mistakes. And Sader knew why one of the dogs had been kept alive.

"Well, could you get him over to the door where I can reach him?"

A little touch of interest seemed to flicker in Ricky's hollow eyes. He nodded slowly.

"Stay there then till I get back."

Sader ran back up the path to the top of the knoll. He remembered what he had seen as he had rested behind one of the great stone heads. Under the night sky he bent and searched the earth, and found what he had expected, rubble tossed out of sight, half-buried in the dead grass, chunks of cement embedded with chicken wire and lathe. He hefted several, finally taking three back with him. They were heavy; his arms ached by the time he reached the house.

He went to the window. Bruce had lain down again, flank against the small body of the boy. When he saw Sader at the window he got to his feet and stretched his neck and showed his teeth and Sader recognized it: *first warning*. This was the spot where the normally nosy person would fade away. Sader rattled the knob and Bruce looked at Ricky as if to say, *Now stay here while I attend to business*.

"Come and unlock the door," Sader said.

Ricky got carefully to his feet, and he and the dog went through the routine again, the dog trying to stay between the child and the door and Ricky leading him past by his ears, evading him. But when Ricky put up a hand to touch the lock, the dog gave a hoarse savage bark and snapped at him. Ricky leaped in fright, and Sader thought, Well, this ends this idea.

Ricky stood there shaking, his face like chalk. Sader couldn't think of anything to do next, outside of smashing the pane and luring the dog to attack him through the window. He hated to risk the noise.

Ricky suddenly calmed, as if in the emergency he knew he had to keep control. Slowly, talking meanwhile to the brute in his piping voice, Ricky slid off the top of his pajamas and dangled it at the dog. Bruce growled and seized the cloth in his teeth. His attitude was at once savage and playful, as if he'd been given a substitute to maul and meant to show what he could do. He pulled, and the pajamas tore, and he shifted his teeth with a snap, to get a better grip. Meanwhile Ricky was moving around so that his back was close to the door. He reached behind him, above his head, his hand out of Sader's sight. But Sader heard the faint clatter of the moving lock. He saw something, too; he saw the dark scars of the beatings across Ricky's back.

Sader had put down two of the chunks. Now he dropped the third, took off his coat, wrapped his left arm in it, picked up the lump of cement and edged his right foot into the slowly opening door. "Get away now, Ricky. He might bite you."

Ricky dropped the pajamas and hurried to the middle of the room. Sader put his left arm across his face and throat, the coat trailing. Bruce dropped the torn pajamas, turned to look; the expression of surprise at Sader's appearance was almost human, almost comical—except for the fangs. He jumped, he got his teeth into the coat. Sader felt the pressure all the way through to his injured wrist. He took a swipe at Bruce with the cement chunk, and the big dog weaved. The chunk slid off the loose skin of his big neck.

Sader thought, Hell, this is old stuff to him, and I'm a goddam amateur.

The dog yanked, throwing all of his weight, and Sader was caught off balance and stumbled forward. The sill caught his foot, and he tripped. He heard Ricky yelling, but he was too busy to look; he had to keep that left arm up, keep Bruce from getting at his throat. The big dog's nose kept pressing closer, his breath hot in Sader's face, and Sader knew that in another minute Bruce was going to let go of the wrapped arm and snap for the jugular vein. He got a better heft on the chunk of cement and took another lick, and this one got Bruce over the ear and made him growl, and that was all. The loose, slick-haired skin shed blows as if Sader was wielding a feather.

Sader saw what had to be done. He rolled on his back on the floor and spread his legs and when Bruce stepped in over him, he clamped his knees upward. Bruce grunted, and growled again, and let go of the arm and dived for Sader's throat. Sader threw the coat upward, clamped it tight with both arms.

The dog's body was like a jumping steel spring. Sader bumped around over the floor, barely hanging on. Then they got into a corner and because he could see where he was and Bruce couldn't, Sader wedged the dog in half-under a carved chest, where he could work on him.

There was nothing about the job that made Sader feel good. It was a cold matter of kill or be killed. He pounded the dog's skull through the coat, and when the big body quit jumping he had to give a couple of extra blows to be sure, and they were the ones he hated.

Then he stood up, weaving, feeling the sweat that had soaked him. He jerked his coat free; it was hot and heavy with the dog's blood. He didn't look at the beaten head. He said to Ricky, "Okay, let's go."

"Don't I need a jacket?"

"We'd better get out of here. I've got a beach blanket in the back of my car."

Ricky came over, hesitating a little, then put his hand shyly in Sader's.

"Are you scared?" Sader asked, wondering what the kid felt about all of this, the dog beaten to death and him standing here soaked and shaking. But Ricky shook his head no.

Sader lifted the boy, carrying the stained coat so it didn't touch him, and went to the door. He listened again for any sound of alarm, took a last look at the room. The carved, ornate Oriental stuff had been gathered from far places, but the effect was heavy; Sader decided he didn't like it. Whether the sculptor, or Wanda's cousin, or whoever—it had been a mistake.

He went out into the dark. The night felt cool on his wet skin. He carried Ricky up the knoll, past the big heads, and Ricky said, "They're awfully starey-eyed, aren't they?" Sader agreed. The gaze of the big stone heads seemed to follow, boring holes in his back. He expected the sound of somebody following, couldn't throw off the feeling of apprehension. When he got close to the big barnlike studio he found himself tiptoeing.

At the car, he put Ricky into the seat, then got the blanket out of the trunk, shook it well, wrapped it around the boy.

"What's your name?" Ricky said suddenly.

"Sader."

"Mr. Sader?"

"Why don't you just call me Joe?"

"All right."

Sader pulled out, turned in the canyon road and headed for the beach. He still couldn't believe that it hadn't been a trap, that he had actually found the boy and gotten him away. The whole thing had the smell of a trap, and there was something more—the instincts he had learned to trust over the years. Somebody must know by now that Sader was operating. The murder of Wanda Nevins showed that. And if that somebody had felt that Sader was anywhere near the truth, his number was up. Up for action.

If the hillside cabin hadn't been the spot where the trap was laid, there was an inevitable conclusion. The real trap was somewhere else.

Sader drove for a while, then glanced over at Ricky. The little boy had curled himself into the blanket and lay there sleeping. Looking at the tousled hair, Sader's mouth tightened. One thing he'd make sure of before anything else happened—he'd make sure that Ricky was in safe hands, past the reach of those who had kept him.

The only lights that burned in Tiffany Square were those on the stone lampposts. They were lantern-shaped, with amber glass, and left everything farther away than three feet in darkness. Sader carried Ricky, still wrapped in the blanket. He went up the steps to Mr. Gibbings' front door. He pulled the iron ring, and the bell clanged indoors.

He waited, shifting the boy's weight. His left arm hurt like hell.

Pretty soon there was the rattle of a chain, and the door opened a little bit. There was a dim light inside. He could make out Irene, in a white nightcap and a fuzzy black robe. "Who is it? My goodness, it's you!" she said.

"It sure is, and I've got to see Mr. Gibbings."

"I don't believe he's in to you now, sir."

"Ask him if he'll be in to Mrs. Champlain's orphan."

He had to repeat it before she got it straight. She went away without locking the door, simply leaving it on the chain, and Sader thought that it must prove that she trusted him a little. Ricky was getting heavy. Sader braced his arm against the lintel.

When she came back, she let the chain down and stepped back. "Mr. Gibbings hasn't felt too well since you were here, and the doctor has put him to bed. He has to stay in it. Will you come this way, please?"

They went up the thick-carpeted old stairs to a wide second-floor hall. The walls were papered with red-and-gold wallpaper, and the runner was old and silky. She opened a door. A single light burned in the big room, and there was Gibbings in a huge bed, under a Turkey-red canopy. He looked fiercely alive, as if something the doctor had said might have insulted him. He growled from under the white mustache: "Well, goddamit, come in as long as you've forced your way here!"

Sader resented the idea he could have browbeat Irene, but this was a time to be humble. He went in, carrying his burden. "I've found the little boy."

"So I see. Irene, you can get out now. But stay close. We want you to take charge of the boy." Gibbings hiked himself up on the mound of pillows. The mustaches took on a livelier angle. "Now. What's this all about, Sader?"

Sader told him. He minimized the part about wrestling the dog, but Gibbings ran an eye over him and said, "Must have been a big brute. You were in a real scrap from the looks of it. You're in your shirt sleeves. What'd he do with your coat?"

Sader told him what had happened to the coat. "I had to bring it along, I couldn't leave it there."

"You mean, there's a cleaning bill?" Gibbings asked sarcastically.

"Look, I'm not asking for a damned thing for myself. No, not even for the fee. I want to put this kid down and let you look at him."

Gibbings had narrowed his eyes. "He looks starved."

"He's been beaten, too."

Sader laid the sleeping child on the foot of the bed and he and old man Gibbings peeled back the blanket and looked at the scarred back.

"It proves that the letter wasn't a lie," Sader pointed out, "but then, you were always convinced it wasn't. But more important—"

Ricky had stirred, was sitting up, rubbing his exhausted small fists into his eyes.

"—more important, does Ricky resemble Mrs. Champlain?"

Gibbings bent, squinting at Ricky, and Ricky drew back from the fierce white mustaches.

"By God. . . ." Gibbings began with enthusiasm, but his voice dwindled. "I started to say yes. It's the coloring, the dark hair, the eyes."

"The features?"

"You know—" Gibbings had curled his lips; his teeth showed. "—if she hadn't had that husband with her, that re-spectable stiff-neck with his polite way and his fishy eye—"

Sader waited, wondering what piece of the puzzle might drop now.

"—I'd have said she could be a hell cat. There was that look about her."

"Thanks," said Sader dryly. "Can you have Irene take charge of Ricky now? Let him sleep, and then feed him, and then have a doctor look him over? I've got to go and see a man about a trap."

CHAPTER EIGHTEEN

The trap existed; Sader was as convinced of it as if he'd seen it planned. When Irene let him out the front door, he stopped there in the dark to light a cigarette, and he sensed the tentacles of other minds hunting for him, a feeling almost as tangible as the clinging of a spider's web. He got into the car and drove back toward Long Beach, the need for sleep grainy and stinging in his eyes, and he tried to figure what they might be doing. If they looked for him in the phone book or the city directory they'd find the office address and the place where he lived, deserted now since he'd been taking care of Scarborough's house.

It might be one of the two. Or it might be anywhere, some dark street, some place he might be expected to revisit—God knew why—or the hillside studio, though if the trap were there he couldn't understand why it hadn't sprung when he went for Ricky.

He drove to his apartment. It was dark. He went in and turned on the lights and looked around, and thought as usual what a lousy housekeeper he was. The mantel clock had run down, and the absence of its throaty ticking made the place seem dead. The tables were dusty. But there was no one waiting, not even in the broom closet, where a yellow-headed mop gave him a momentary start.

He thought to himself, they wouldn't be at the office. Not now. There was no reason he should go there. And the answering service would give a caller Scarborough's phone number but not the address; he'd be perfectly safe there. It was a time to go to bed. He closed the door and headed for Los Alamitos.

The tires crunched on the gravel drive, and Sader got out, shut the garage door and turned to the house. A jet went over on some night maneuver or other, shaking the ground he walked on. The airfield lights lit up the sky. Sader took out the key Scarborough had given him, went up the rear steps, fitted the key into the back door. And then, inside the house, the dog whined.

Sader stopped with his hand on the knob.

Every previous night that he'd come here the dog had barked when he had heard him on the porch, had jumped against the other side of the door, frantic with happiness that the substitute master had come at last and that he was to be fed and let out to run.

Sader stepped back to the edge of the porch and listened. The dog didn't whine again. Sader whistled, sharply. Nothing answered but the silence.

Sader crossed the porch to the wall, stretched his arm, reinserted the key and turned it, yanked the door wide. There was still no further sound from the setter, but something came out. An odor, a hint of fragrance. Perfume. Sader put his mouth close to the doorway and said, "What have you got? A gun?"

He thought he could hear stifled laughter. There was more than one of them. Sader's look was grim. He stepped off the porch without a sound, went out to the car. It was time to even the odds. He took the Police Positive out of the locked glove compartment, shut the compartment, went down the other side of the driveway where his feet made no sound on the grass, crossed the drive and went to the front door. He was hoping as he went that they hadn't done anything to the dog. Scarborough was crazy about the setter.

He opened the door without a sound and slid in, stopped in the dark to get his bearings. He could make out the dim shapes of furniture, the blank aperture of the door opposite, the door leading to the hall and the stairs and the rear part of the house.

Walking silently, Sader went into the hall. Here he again caught the scent of perfume, a subtle and musky fragrance, and he realized why it seemed so noticeable—the house smelled of its everyday occupants, Scarborough's scrupulously clean little old aunt and Scarborough's rum-and-maple pipe tobacco. Sader went to the kitchen doorway and looked through. The door he had yanked open still swung wide, and against the reflected glow outside he could see their figures, a man and a woman. Sader said, "Why don't you put on the lights?"

They turned swiftly, and the woman gave a small cry.

Sader reached inside the door to click the switch.

The man was what he expected, husky and young, tanned, blond hair cut in a crewcut, dressed in brown slacks and a plaid tan jacket, very expensive looking. He had a leather sap in his hand, hanging by a leather thong. Sader looked at it and felt goose flesh growing along his arms. Without a doubt it was what had been used on Wanda Nevins.

He looked at the woman, dark and exotic, her eyes alive with fury. "Stupid of me to have thought you'd have a gun," Sader said thoughtfully. "The only gun used so far in this thing was old man Perrine's rifle. He took a pot shot at his son. They've been arguing over you . . . Mrs. Champlain."

Her face convulsed.

"But of course, a gun isn't your way. You have your young friend here, who will do anything for money—even to disposing of a blackmailing cousin. By the way, when his time came, how were you going to get rid of him?"

"I'm not . . . I'm not Tina Champlain!"

"Should we test that statement?" Sader wondered. "Say, on someone like Mrs. Cecil?"

"You must be crazy." She was actually laughing at him. "I'm Tina's sister. I stepped in and took charge of her child when she drowned, and now I'm settling her estate. And there are . . . details that could be spoiled by someone meddling. Like you." She paused; her eyes held Sader's glitteringly and he saw what he was almost unwilling to see, that reason had left her, and he understood then what Brent Perrine had been angry about when he had said she'd gone overboard. She had—overboard into madness.

"Probably you do feel like a sister of the woman you once were, or almost anyone except yourself," Sader agreed. "You've changed, of course. There are things you do now that you must really not like to think about. Don't like to believe are happening." Sader threw a glance at the man. Under the blond crewcut the face had grown mask-like with a look of concentration, and the right hand had moved a trifle. "If you lift that sap an inch I'll shoot you right in the gut."

The blond man licked his lips.

"I won't let you get behind me as you did Wanda."

There was taut silence between the three of them.

Sader turned to the woman. "Your husband loved you. He loved you a lot. Since his job took him all over the world, he gathered treasures for you and brought them home . . . all the stuff you have hidden in that canyon house at Laguna. But there was one thing he couldn't give you. I imagine you demanded. You wanted a child, and he couldn't provide."

She tried to look away. For an instant Sader thought that she would come out of the nightmare, or dream, or obsession, or whatever had her in its grip. Her eyes grew gentle, the hard lines smoothed from around her mouth. But then the look faded.

He pressed on. "You were determined to have a child, and being the kind of woman you are, you tried to goad him by taunting. You made his life miserable, and your own. Things must have been about at the breaking point. And then something totally unexpected happened. You went to the mountain cabin near Tehachapi and there you ran into somebody–probably you're telling yourself even yet that it was rape. I'll bet it's what you told Champlain. You found out you were pregnant and you made plans to keep the child, but he wouldn't let you. You were moody and distraught, you dropped all your friends, but he made you go away anyway, go to a private sanitarium to have the baby. Your aunt knows this much."

She made a harsh, breathy attempt to laugh at him again. "My aunt doesn't know a damned thing about it."

"She's a good guesser. Let me try guessing, too. You had the baby and you let Wanda help you put it out for adoption, and then your husband let you take another baby in its place. A baby he could look at without being reminded of what you'd done to him." Sader was studying her features under the bright overhead light. Under normal conditions she must be rather beautiful. The face was finely made, the dark eyes brilliant under thick lashes, the lips full. "You had the baby girl, and you tried to take up the old life again, the quiet respectable life as Champlain's wife, but your heart wasn't in it. Champlain's death gave you the money and the baby's death gave you the chance–for freedom."

"What's it matter to you?" the cousin said suddenly. "What're you sticking your nose in for?"

"When I want any remarks from you I'll ask for them," Sader said.

Tina Champlain walked stiff-legged to a kitchen chair and slid down into it. She clasped her hands in a sudden motion of frailty, with her gaze fixed on Sader; she seemed to wait in dread for him to go on.

Sader gave her a lopsided grin. "I'd say that the man you met in the mountains was somebody you didn't care to see again. Maybe a kind of drifter, a hitchhiker, a tramp. Not even in the same class with your husband. But full of animal strength and vitality."

She brushed at the hair that was matted with sweat at her temples. "He . . . he sufficed."

"He provided you with a revenge against your inadequate husband," Sader agreed. "And probably you had the idea you could take Ricky back, take your own child home again, without any onrush of guilty complexes. Only it didn't work out that way. You had had, after all, a good religious upbringing, and then old man Perrine kept nosing at the relationship, reminding you how the boy resembled you, and when you looked at Ricky you began to see not him, but the man who had had you. You saw the face and the form of the man with whom you had betrayed your husband. You began to abuse the child—Mrs. Cecil remembered that he had begun to grow thin—and when you saw that the abuse was going to get out of control, you arranged the drowning. You paid a price, a good one, and the Perrines kept your secret."

Wanda's cousin must have thought that Sader's attention was completely centered on the woman, for he chose that moment to act. The upswing was quick and venomous, the leather sap seemed to explode with menace under the glow of the overhead light, and Sader knew that the next moment this combination of muscle and nerve and shot-weighted sap was going to crush him to the floor and beat him to a pulp. But in that moment his gun splintered the quiet. The lifted brawny arm came down with a rush, there was still plenty of control, plenty of power, though in the instant before the sap struck Sader's arm a strange light seemed to pass over the other man's face, and there was shock in the depths of his pale eyes.

His knees shuddered together and locked, one above the other, the sap dropped to the floor, and then he tumbled down face first, grabbing at his midsection with a cry of rage and surprise.

She leaped off the chair like a cat. But the scream she gave didn't resemble anything alive, it wasn't even animal, it was a noise like a steel blade on stone, or an iron wheel being dragged along a track, or a flywheel that needed oil. She hit Sader in a flurry of fists and claws, and even in the midst of the buffeting he was aware of her scent, strong and clovelike. He tried to fend her off, tried to pry away her flailing and digging hands, and then something went wrong. The gun went off again, though he hadn't meant it to.

She stepped back. One shoulder hung crooked and she was bent a little at the waist.

Sader stood there aghast, not believing it had happened.

She turned to look at the writhing man on the floor. "Jeffry?"

He was past listening to her. He was wrapped in his own torment, his own struggle to live. He was trying to hold life inside him by wrapping his arms so tightly across his middle that it couldn't get away.

Her shoulder dropped a little farther and then her whole torso tilted, her throat relaxing and her face turned to the ceiling. The way her knees bent reminded Sader of the breaking of a straw. She fell to the floor and lay still. Sader dropped the gun on a chair and bent over her, trying to see where she was hit. The suit was a soft black wool, loosely woven, and the bullet had gone in without making a mark. He couldn't believe at first that she was shot; the bullet had gone wild.

Then the bubbles began to come up with her breathing, and they were crimson. Sader bent closer. "Can you talk? There may not be much time left."

She looked at him calmly. "Ricky. . . ."

"Ricky's safe . . . beyond your ever getting again."

The dark eyes flickered. "I loved him." Sader grimaced, and she insisted. "But I did, I really did. He is a very lovable little boy. It was just . . . after a while, I couldn't forget. I kept thinking about my husband, and then I found that I was seeing Ricky the way *he* saw him. Something left over from a dark and dirty secret."

"What a horrible attitude to take toward your child."

"Some days," she whispered, "I let him call me Mother, and I loved him, I fed him."

Her eyes were glazing. "You should have left him with whoever had him those first three years. Or given him to someone when you changed toward him. There are people everywhere who want children, who are dying to have children." Sader slapped her cheek lightly and the eyes opened, but only for a moment. "You didn't love him, ever. You hated him."

Her lips fluttered with her breath. "Hate is . . . hate is the other side of the coin," she said.

Sader rose to his feet. "Just stay there. I'm going to call a doctor."

His shadow fell across her like a foretaste of dark.

By the time the doctor and the ambulance reached the house, Tina Champlain was dead. Jeffry, the cousin, was still alive and the doctor looked him over and decided that there was a chance he might make it. Sader had phoned Jackson in Santa Ana, and the Sheriff's man wanted to question Jeffry about Wanda's murder as soon as he got there, but the doctor wouldn't let him.

The ambulance took away Tina's body, the moaning man, and then Jackson sat down at the kitchen table and let Sader pour him a cup of coffee.

Sader prowled around until he located the dog, stuffed into a closet with some mops and cleaning paraphernalia, and let him out. The dog jumped around until Sader fed him. Then the parrot squawked and Sader had to take the black hood off the cage.

Over the coffee, Jackson growled at Sader, "You don't look like much of a tomcat, but damned if you don't have nine lives."

"I know I'm lucky to be here," Sader said, sitting down across the table. "Those two were pretty cute. They killed Wanda when she got too nosy, they were ready to kill me, too. They'd followed me here, some other time, and then tonight they set their trap and waited. It was just a fluke I heard the dog whine, I didn't walk in here and meet that sap in the dark."

Sader lighted a cigarette while he thought about it, re-membering how sure he had been that the trap wouldn't be laid at Scarborough's place because no one knew he was living here.

Jackson too had lighted a cigarette, but now he crushed it out in a burst of anger. "I can't believe she'd do all this, pretend to drown, and hide, and set up that hidden place you say she had in Laguna canyon, just to have her way with a kid."

"I think Brent Perrine summed it up. He said she went overboard. She did just that. She let herself be swamped by emotions she couldn't control. Remember the kind of girl she'd been, according to her aunt—a wild one. The neighbors gossiping. Then she was able to flaunt a respectable marriage to Champlain in their faces. He must have been quite a catch in her circle. And then at the end, there she was alone with her illegitimate child. And so she took out her rage and her shame in punishing Ricky."

"Then all she felt for the kid was hate."

"Oh, no. She did *love* Ricky, too. No doubt even while she was beating and starving him, there were times of tenderness. And then, remember this: she was the one who wrote the letter to Gibbings."

Jackson jerked up his head and stared at Sader as if Sader were coming unstuck at the seams. "Now wait a minute—"

"Hell, she was the only one who could have done it."

"But why—"

"In the midst of all that hell, she must have had some hope that somebody would stop her. It couldn't have been fun, driven by emotions like hers, driven to do the things she did to the little boy. She had to have some hope of change, some chance of capture. And so she wrote the letter to the only person she figured had the money and the power to find her. And she put in the deliberate lie, that the baby was Gibbings' grandchild, so that he wouldn't ever think it might be her. A devious trick, but reasonable when you understand what she was doing."

"Wait. If she wanted to be caught, if she really wanted Ricky to be saved, then why have Jeffry murder Wanda? Why not let Wanda tell the truth to Gibbings?"

"Oh, Wanda didn't intend to tell the truth to anybody. She wanted cash to keep her mouth shut. I'm sure that murdering her was Jeffry's idea. He had moved in on Tina, was gradually acquiring almost complete control of her and her money. He knew that Wanda had shaken her down for about forty thousand to relocate Ricky, plus a down payment on the Laguna place. He didn't intend for any more of the money to find its way to Wanda. No doubt in time he meant to get every dime that Tina had left. I think killing me was Jeffry's idea, too. I didn't see any sign of disappointment in Tina when she finally knew it was all over."

Jackson said, "Wait up, you said this was all reasonable when you knew what Tina Champlain was doing. Well, what was she doing?"

"Getting ready to die. In one way or another. Probably intending to take Ricky with her when she thought they'd both had enough of torment."

Jackson rubbed the back of his neck as if something had touched him there, a cold breath that brought up the hairs of his scalp. "A psychiatrist would say that she was insane."

Sader nodded. "I guess so."

"Weren't you stumped when you saw her, when you guessed who she was?"

"Oh, no," Sader said, "I knew who she had to be. Ever since Ricky told me about the woman who had been keeping him. He started to say Mother, and then cut it off; she'd put a stop to that. Then he said that Jeffry called this woman 'Mrs. Lasriss.' And I tried to dig it out, it made me think of that minister, Twining, and something he'd called to mind. Out of the Bible, of course. Jeffry had been calling Tina 'Mrs. Lazarus.' Because she'd risen, so to speak, from the dead."

"What a pair they made!"

"She was sick with a desire to die—but he wasn't. I'll bet when you look around in that canyon house, you find a big wad of cash. I gave some thought to the idea she might have spent most of her money trying to keep the little girl alive, but now I think not. I think after she paid Wanda, and bribed the Perrines, there was still a big chunk left. And it was there where Jeffry could keep an eye on it."

Jackson was staring at Sader. "You've made quite a case. But it will take some proving. The Grand Jury's apt to wonder if you didn't get these two people out here and shoot them for some reason of your own."

"Oh, hell, there's still work to be done."

CHAPTER NINETEEN

Sader phoned Twining early the next morning, explained what had happened, and asked if Twining would call the former pastor, Dr. Bell, at once. Then Sader drove into Long Beach to his office, and tried to catch up on some work. He knew that Jackson would be busy on the Laguna end.

Twining called within a half-hour. Dr. Bell would be flying out for the inquest.

"Dr. Bell knew all about Mrs. Champlain's child," Twining told Sader. "She went to Dr. Bell almost as soon as she knew that she was pregnant. She wanted him to help her persuade Champlain that they could keep the baby. Champlain was adamant. He was even thinking of divorcing her, though she swore to Dr. Bell that the pregnancy was due to a rape, that she had done nothing to encourage the man, didn't know him, never expected to see him again. The way Dr. Bell put it was this: she had a quirk of being attracted to violent people."

Remembering the crewcut cousin, Sader said, "She sure did."

"Champlain said some pretty ugly things to her in front of Dr. Bell. Dr. Bell thinks they struck pretty deep."

"They prepared the way for what happened to Ricky."

"Yes. It was Dr. Bell's suggestion, by the way, that led them to look for another baby. He still believes that if Champlain hadn't died in that plane crash, and if the baby girl had lived, there would have been no trouble. But when all that happened, when she decided to break away from her old life and take Ricky back—he knew that she was headed for disaster. There was simply nothing he could do."

"Perhaps if he hadn't gone away—"

Twining's voice was regretful. "She had long since refused to listen to anything he had to say."

An hour later Jackson was on the line, telling Sader that they had picked up Brent Perrine at the Mexican border, and got the truth about Tina's supposed drowning. There had been friction over the money Tina had paid them to keep their mouths shut, the old man wanted it for booze and Brent was blaming him now for his predicament. "He's afraid we're trying to pin Wanda Nevins' murder on him. He keeps telling us he didn't see Tina more than a couple of times after she sneaked away from their boat at Catalina. She'd taken up with some relative of Miss Nevins. Then he tried to give us a line that Tina had dropped from sight to avoid paying inheritance taxes on the money Champlain left her. But of course, when I told him we knew what she'd been up to, he admitted it. He said it gave him the creeps, knowing what she wanted with the little boy, and that he hunted for the kid in the canyon house, where he ran into you."

"It could be. Keep him on the fire about the murder and you might get more."

But in the end it was Jeffry, the cousin, who cleared up the last details. He was in the hospital, undergoing his third transfusion, when he suddenly began to sink. The doctor called Jackson in at once, and the blond man confessed to killing Wanda.

Wanda had accepted the story of Tina's drowning, until Sader had come asking questions. Then her curiosity had been stirred and she had done some snooping, and remembering her cousin's liking for Tina, Wanda had followed him, had found out that Tina was alive and was living with Jeffry in the canyon house. Then Wanda had requested fifty thousand—for a start.

He had beaten her to death in her bedroom, had sapped one of the dogs. He had taken the other dog with him—it had always been friendly—and he thought that he and Tina could use a watchdog.

After Sader heard about it from Jackson, he tried to call Gibbings. Gibbings wasn't in his office, and Irene at home said stiffly that Mr. Gibbings was out. This went on for almost a week, and Sader had begun to think of making a trip to Tiffany Square, when suddenly Gibbings phoned him. "Gibbings here. I've called about your fee," he began without preamble. "I suppose you've added it all up and so on."

"I've been thinking about it. I've decided there's just one fee I want out of all this, and that is the care and raising of one Ricky Champlain, in a good home."

The old man cackled, and Sader's mind pictured him as he'd first seen him, iron-eyed and with those mettlesome mustaches, the tiny teeth and manner of a tyrant—and inside somewhere a core of decency and concern for a child that he had tried to cover up. "I knew you'd say that, dammit, I knew it!" Gibbings crowed. "But we're way ahead of you here, Ricky's got his own room, all new clothes and a bicycle, and my daughter hardly lets him out of her sight."

"That's a fair trade for her," Sader said evenly.

It took the old man aback but only for a moment. "You'd say so. Anyway, we took Ricky to the best pediatrician in town, and he says the boy's going to be fine. Just needs good food and plenty of rest, and somebody to keep an eye on him."

Sader was yanking a cigarette from a pack with his free hand. "I don't have to worry about Ricky any more."

"No, sir, you don't." Gibbings hung up as Sader was getting the cigarette lighted.

This was the end of the affair, really the end—and then Sader thought of one thing more. He rummaged in the desk, found it, the baby's mitten with its touch of pink. He had to dispose of this tag end. He had promised the woman at the baby shop to send it back. But now he shook his head at this idea.

Finally he typed up an envelope addressed to Kit Gibbings at her home, wrapped the mitten in a sheet of typing paper and sealed it in the envelope, went downstairs to mail it.

He dropped it into the corner mailbox. When he turned, his eye fell on the entrance of a bar. There was a neon sign COCKTAILS and the green outline of a martini glass that tilted back and forth. Of course he wouldn't go in for a drink. It was still early afternoon. Not only that, there was no use fooling himself about what would happen. He had no control. One drink would be the start of a drunk, and tomorrow's hangover would be horrendous.

He ought to call Twining, come to think of it. Ministers were supposed to help you fight off such impulses.

But suddenly he craved to sit at a bar and look peacefully into a bar mirror, and find the taste of whiskey in his mouth, and think. To think deeply of all that had happened.

Most of the people who hired him were here today and gone tomorrow, a series of shadows with grimly personal puzzles for him to share. But in this thing, the people had been unforgettable.

He wanted to drink a toast to Wanda, for one. She had been gorgeous and thoroughly mercenary, and now she was dead.

He wanted to drink a toast to Tina, who had died twice.

He wanted to drink a toast to Ricky, because in his own way he had shown a supreme courage in the middle of hell.

Most of all he wanted to toast Kit Gibbings, who had been an unwed mother and who had lain down unnumbered nights to sleep with slander, and who had kept right on being a lady.

He went into the bar and slid upon the stool and said to the bald bartender, "Bourbon and soda. Better make it a triple." The bartender nodded and put away his racing form.

In the bar mirror, Sader's reflection looked back at him, gray-eyed and drawn, weary, and Sader stared at it closely and began to think.

ABOUT DOLORES HITCHENS AND STEPH CHA

In a 1952 letter to her editor at Doubleday, Dolores Hitchens wryly explained that her full name, thanks to "a series of step-fathers and two husbands," was "Julia Clara Catherine Maria Dolores Robins Norton Birk Olsen Hitchens." She was born in San Antonio, Texas, on December 25, 1907, her parents W. H. Robbins and Myrtle (Statham) Robbins "of pioneer Texas stock." She later remembered her great-great-grandmother as "the first woman to step on Texas soil with Austin's colony," and her grandfather as "a sheriff during the wild-and-woolly period." She spent her grammar school years in the "oil-field country" of Kern County, California, her father dying while she was an infant and her mother subsequently divorcing a second husband. In 1922, the family moved to Long Beach, California, where her mother married Oscar Carl Birk and where Julia Birk (as Hitchens was then called) went to high school. Her literary career began during her high school years, with the publication of stories and poems in *The Long Beach Press* and the sale of a short poem to *Motion Picture Magazine*, where it appeared in July 1924.

After graduation, now calling herself Dolores Birk, Hitchens attended UCLA and worked in nearby Seal Beach for two years as a third-grade teacher. On August 3, 1931, at twenty-three, she married Beverley S. Olsen, a ship's purser and radio operator, in San Francisco; they moved in with her parents, and on July 5, 1935, had a daughter, Patricia Marie. Three years later, as D. B. Olsen, Hitchens published her first novel, *The Clue in the Clay*; the following year, in 1939, she published a second novel featuring its detective protagonist Lieutenant Stephen Mayhew, *Death Cuts a Silhouette*, and then *Cat Saw Murder*, the first novel in what would become her popular, twelve-novel series of "cat" mysteries centered around spinster-detective Rachel Murdock.

Hitchens divorced Olsen to marry Hubert A. Hitchens, an investigator for the Southern Pacific Railroad Police and the father of two teenage sons, in late 1940 or 1941. On July 18, 1942, they had a son of their own, Michael John. She enjoyed "cooking elaborate dishes, dabbling in sculpture, raising fancy chickens, and traveling in a 'jalopy,'" according to a biographical sketch published in 1943. She took psychology courses at a local college, "with the ultimate aim of outfitting my characters with the latest in psychoses and fixations." The new family lived in and around Long Beach for the next sixteen years, with some time spent in the Northern California town of Eureka in the late 1940s. Her daughter Patricia married in 1952. In 1955, with her husband and son, she vacationed in Havana.

While she continued to write novels and magazine stories under her nom de plume D. B. Olsen—including a six-volume series of mysteries featuring English literature professor A. Pennyfeather, and a 1962 western, *The Night of the Bowstring*—her new name gave Hitchens "a fresh lease on life" and "a new reincarnation, book-wise." Moving away from D. B. Olsen's cozier, more domestic style, the novels of Dolores Hitchens—including *Stairway to an Empty Room* (1951), *Nets to Catch the Wind* (1952), *Terror Lurks in Darkness* (1953), *Beat Back the Tide* (1954), the James Sader mysteries *Sleep with Strangers* (1955) and *Sleep with Slander* (1960), and *Fool's Gold* (1958), the last adapted by French New Wave director Jean-Luc Godard for his 1964 film *Bande à part* (*Band of Outsiders*)—are increasingly suspenseful and hard-boiled thrillers. She also wrote novels under the pseudonyms Dolan Birkley and Noel Burke, and she collaborated with Bert Hitchens on an innovative series of railroad police procedurals that included *F.O.B. Murder* (1955), *One-Way Ticket* (1956), *End of the Line* (1957), *The Man Who Followed Women* (1959), and *The Grudge* (1963).

Divorcing her husband in 1959, Hitchens moved to an apartment in nearby Anaheim. Her later Dolores Hitchens novels include *The Watcher* (1959), *Footsteps in the Night* (1961), *The Abductor* (1962), *The Bank with the Bamboo Door* (1965), *The Man Who Cried All the Way Home* (1966), *Postscript to Nightmare* (1967), *A Collection of Strangers* (1969), *The Baxter Letters* (1971), and *In a House Unknown* (1973). She died at sixty-five on August 1, 1973, and was buried in Holy Sepulcher Cemetery in Orange, California.

*

Steph Cha is the author of *Your House Will Pay*, winner of the *Los Angeles Times* Book Prize and the California Book Award, and the Juniper Song crime trilogy. She's a critic whose work has appeared in the *Los Angeles Times*, *USA Today*, and the *Los Angeles Review of Books*, where she served as noir editor, and is the current series editor of the *Best American Mystery & Suspense* anthology. A native of the San Fernando Valley, she lives in Los Angeles with her family.